Albert Aiken

The brigand captain

The prairie pathfinder

Albert Aiken

The brigand captain
The prairie pathfinder

ISBN/EAN: 9783337197476

Printed in Europe, USA, Canada, Australia, Japan

Cover: Foto ©Andreas Hilbeck / pixelio.de

More available books at **www.hansebooks.com**

Price 5d.] [No. 9.

ROMANCES FOR THE MILLION

The BRIGAND CAPTAIN

OR, THE PRAIRIE PATHFINDER.

General Publishing Company, 280, Strand.

THE
BRIGAND CAPTAIN:

OR, THE

PRAIRIE PATHFINDER.

BY

CAPTAIN W. AIKEN.

LONDON :
OFFICE OF THE "ILLUSTRATED LONDON NOVELETTE,"
280, STRAND, W.C.

THE
BRIGAND CAPTAIN;

OR,

THE PRAIRIE PATHFINDER.

CHAPTER I.
IN THE JAWS OF DEATH.

ALONG the bank of the Rio Grande—the river that separates the State of Texas from the Republic of Mexico—walked a young man. The double-barrelled shot-gun carried upon his shoulder proclaimed him in search of game; the dress of the hunter- the whiteness of his skin—told that he was an American. Besides, he was on the Texan side of the river. In person the sportsman was a tall, well-built young fellow; possibly five-and-twenty years had passed over his head; his face was of the Anglo-Saxon type; light yellow hair curled in little ringlets tight to his head; his eyes were dark blue, approaching a grey in tint, save when the sunlight shone upon them; a moustache and little imperial of the same tawny hue as the hair graced his lip and chin; his features were regular and pleasing, and the squareness of the chin told of firmness and self-reliance. For dress, the hunter wore the blue uniform of Uncle

R 2

Sam, and the single bar upon his shoulder told that he held the rank of lieutenant in the army of the Republic.

It was evident that the officer was not on duty, for he was without sword or sash, and wore an undress blouse instead of the regular uniform coat.

The bank of the river was fringed with timber, and from the timber extended, inland, the prairie—a rolling one, fragrant with tall grass and many-hued flowers, for it was in the pleasant month of June.

As yet the hunter had roused neither bird nor beast to test his marksmanship; still on he went up the stream. At last he came to where a little creek —now nearly dry—ran from the prairie into the river. It required but a moderate jump to span it, and, as the other bank looked firm and solid the sportsman determined to leap across. So, nerving himself for the effort, he sprung over. The leap was a good one, and he struck fairly upon the low, yellow bank opposite, and found himself up to his knees in mud.

"The deuce!" he cried, in vexation. "This is a nice pickle. I've got more than I bargained for."

He attempted to draw his legs from the mire and gain the firm ground, but, on making the effort he found, to his astonishment, that he was unable to move an inch; his feet and legs seemed glued in the soft earth. Then, to his horror, he became conscious that he was gradually sinking, and the truth flashed upon him—he was in a quicksand. Though he had often heard of such spots yet this was the first one he ever had seen. Slowly, little by little, he felt the ground giving way beneath him, and it soon became evident that, unless he could contrive some means to escape, the United States army would be one lieutenant the less in an hour's time.

What was to be done? No trees or bushes were within reach. As a first expedient, he fired off both barrels of his gun in quick succession; the sound might attract someone to his aid, but travellers along the bank of the Rio Grande were few and far between. Some herdsman scouring the prairie in quest of cattle possibly might hear the reports, yet there was but one chance out of a hundred that he would seek for the cause.

Inch by inch the young officer felt himself sinking into his grave. He was, indeed, in the "jaws of death." Vainly he tried to throw himself over on his side so as to oppose more resistance to the action of the treacherous morass, but the quicksand clung around his legs with a giant's power.

In agony the young soldier groaned aloud. He was a brave man—had won his grade on the bloody fields of the Mexican war, then but a few years past —had faced death at the cannon's mouth—had sought for it amid Canolles' glittering lances—had escaped all the perils of the battle-field to perish now so horribly—to be swallowed up in the maw of the bottomless quicksand!

The banks of the little stream, like those of the Rio Grande, being fringed with bushes, shut from the eyes of the soldier the view of the distant prairie. Assistance might be passing at any moment and yet the soldier, unable to see, could give no warning of his awful position.

The quicksand had reached his waist; at the rate he had been sinking, an hour more would bring it above his head.

Desperately and almost without hope the imprisoned man cried for help. The prairie winds bore back the echo of his voice and seemed to mock his despair.

At last, hoarse with shouting and almost frantic with agony, the young man resigned himself to his seemingly inevitable fate.

Still he sunk. The surface of the quicksand had reached his breast. The little glade which, when he entered it, seemed so fresh in its beauty, now wore to him the aspect of a tomb. He watched with painful intensity the yellow wall rising so steadily around him; he counted the moments when those sands would enter his mouth and choke the breath from his body. The agony of such a death was appalling, even in the anticipation of it.

Then he thought of the wonder of his comrades when his absence should be discovered that night; of the search that would be made, and fruitlessness of that search.

"I shall disappear from the world utterly," he said, bitterly. "Well, there is none to mourn much for me. Oh! why didn't I fall in Mexico gloriously, instead of dying here, the death of a dog?"

Then to the listening ears of the doomed man came a sound rolling over the broad expanse of the prairie —a sound that caused his heart to beat quicker—his blood, almost stilled in its flow by the near approach of the grim king of terrors, to leap wildly in his veins. And what was that sound?—the sound that promised hope and help to the death-encircled man? It was the clear-ringing "thud," of a horse's hoofs striking the firm earth of the prairie.

Eagerly the young soldier shouted, and the free winds seized upon the hoarse voice and bore it far away over the swells of the rolling prairie.

The minutes were minutes of torture to the helpless man. Would the horseman hear the sound, or would he pass on and leave him to die?

The sound of the hoofs' beat came nearer and

nearer, and each stroke upon the soil raised a new hope in the breast of the sinking man.

Then the heart of the young soldier leaped with joy, for, on the bank of the little creek appeared a horse and rider—the horse a pure cream-coloured mustang —the rider a Mexican girl of surpassing beauty.

The soldier thought at first that an angel from heaven had descended to his aid, but the clear, musi- cal tones of the girl's voice convinced him that she was but mortal.

"Senor, you are in the quicksand!" cried the girl.

"Yes; can you aid me?" asked the soldier.

"Yes, senor, I can save you."

"How?" asked the soldier, anxiously.

"With my lasso," answered the girl, and then she gathered up the leather cord, and with a dexterous throw cast the loop over the young soldier's head.

"Fasten it beneath your arms, senor," she said. "The other end is fast to the horn in my saddle. I will then start my horse and pull you out."

The soldier obeyed the instructions : the girl started her horse with great caution, and, in a minute or so, the young lieutenant stood on the bank of the creek *saved !*

Lieutenant Philip Wenie—for so he was called— had looked on many a beautiful girl in the course of his life, but never in his eyes had girl appeared so lovely as the Mexican maid that had saved him from his terrible danger.

"Are you hurt, senor?" asked the girl, gathering the lasso up into little coils."

"No," returned the lieutenant; "I attempted to jump across the creek and had no idea that the shore was a quicksand."

"You are an American soldier?" asked the girl, glancing at his uniform.

" Yes."

" Do you come from Santa Fe ?"

" Yes, but some time ago. At present I am stationed in the little village yonder," and the soldier pointed down the river.

" Tacos ?" asked the girl, in wonder.

" Yes."

" I did not know any soldiers were stationed at Tacos ; I live scarcely a mile from there," said the girl.

The young officer could not repress a smile of gladness when he discovered that she lived in the neighbourhood.

" Very likely," he said, in reply to her speech. " We came but yesterday."

" And do you intend to stay ?" asked the girl.

" Yes ; for awhile at least."

" I am glad of that !" cried the girl, quickly.

And the lieutenant was glad of it too, although he did not say so. He already was half in love with the girl who had rescued him.

" Then you do not regard Americans as your foes ?" the officer asked.

" No ; why should I ?" replied the girl. " I have never met with anything but kind treatment from them. Besides I am an American too, now, for I live on the Texas side of the Rio Grande, and of course I must love my brothers."

Wenie, as he gazed upon her fair face and sparkling black eyes, in his heart wished that she would extend a little of her love to him.

" You say you live *near* Tacos ?" he asked.

" Yes, only a mile on the El Pasco road. You will come and see me, senor ? My father will be glad to welcome you. My name is Juanita Torres."

" And mine, Philip Wenie, a lieutenant in the

United States army. But I haven't thanked you yet for saving my life. Only for you I should have been buried in yonder quicksand," said the officer, earnestly.

"Oh, please don't speak of that," said Juanita, blushing at the earnest gaze of the young officer; "anyone would have done the same. Besides, my horse did more than I, for I but cast the lasso to you, while he pulled you out; so you see you owe him the thanks, not me."

The lieutenant shook his head gravely.

"I'm afraid that if *you* had not come along with the horse my chances for safety would have been small. I assure you I shall never forget the service, and possibly, some day, I may be able to repay it."

"Now, if you say a single word of thanks, I shall be angry. Are you going to Tacos?" she asked.

"Yes," he answered.

"Well," I go a mile that way with you, and I will point out my father's house to you."

"With pleasure!" cried the lieutenant, delighted at the chance of remaining in her society.

So together they proceeded in the direction of the town.

The lieutenant had the greatest desire in the world to appear to good advantage in the eyes of his fair companion, but, as he was covered to the armpits with the yellow mud of the quicksand, he could not help confessing to himself that he was not in the best possible condition to make an impression upon the heart of a young and handsome girl.

"How came you to discover me in my perilous position?" he asked, as they proceeded slowly along, the girl accommodating the pace of her steed to that of her companion on foot.

"I heard the reports of your gun, and I thought it was the Pathfinder," she answered.

"The Pathfinder?" said the lieutenant, in surprise,

"Yes, senor; Manuel the Pathfinder is my father's chief herdsman. He promised me some game for supper; so, of course, when I heard the shots I thought that it was he, and thinking to surprise him, I rode directly where the sound came from; but there, instead of the herdsman, I found you."

"It was indeed a lucky chance that sent you to my aid. Another half-hour and the quicksand would have closed over my head. I shall never forget the service you have rendered me," said Wenie, warmly.

"Yes; but you must forget it, or at least not speak of it. You will make me think I have done something noble, instead of which I have done nothing but a simple duty. That is my house yonder," and the girl pointed to the left. "Good-by. Remember—come!" and the girl rode off.

Wenie looked after her, his heart in a blaze with passion's fire.

CHAPTER II.
THE EXPEDITION TO TACOS.

THE lieutenant watched the girl until she disappeared in the distance, hid from view by the swells of the rolling prairie; then he continued on his course to the village.

The young man, like all other young men, had fancied himself in love a score of times or more; but never had he seen a woman who had so completely taken possession of his fancy as this fair young Mexican. He determined to follow up the acquaintance thus so strangely begun.

In a short time the lieutenant reached his quarters in the village, changed his clothes, and soon removed all traces of the danger that he had passed.

The village of Tacos was but a collection of a few scattered houses clustered around what had formerly been the mission-house, for, like nearly all the Mexican settlements on the Indian frontier, Tacos had originally been founded by the priests—the men who, with the Bible in one hand and the sword in the other, dared the perils of the wilderness to establish the true faith. But the Mexican revolution, which broke the Spanish yoke, did much to diminish the power of the priesthood, and, after that time, nearly all the frontier missions had been abandoned; so that, when the company of Federal cavalry, sixty strong, filed by fours into Tacos, they found that the old mission-house and its adjoining buildings, with a few repairs, would serve admirably for quarters.

Now, then, what brought a company of United States soldiers to that insignificant valley? True, it was on the Rio Grande, the frontier-line between Mexico and Texas; but as there was peace between the two countries, an "army of observation" was hardly needed. Had you asked the soldiers themselves they could not have answered satisfactorily, but had you put the question to the officer in command of the expedition, Major Curtin, an elderly, grey-haired soldier, a major by brevet, who had greatly distinguished himself during the late war, you would have learned that the cavalry were there to watch the "Brigands of the Prairie."

Who were they?

All along the frontier, from the Gulf of Mexico in the south to the boundary-line of New Mexico in the north, there existed a band of robbers—men bound together by fearful oaths—who depredated alike on Mexican and American soil. The horses or beeves stolen in Mexico would be hastily driven across the Rio Grande to Texan soil and disposed of there; the

plunder procured in Texas or New Mexico would be
taken into Mexico and sold there.   The actual number of the band—that is, those who did the plunder-
ing—was supposed not to exceed thirty, but it was
currently reported that they had confederates—men
high in reputation among their neighbours, men of
wealth and settled position—on both sides of the Rio
Grande, who aided the robbers in their escape from
justice, and assisted them in disposing of their ill-
gotten booty.   So formidable had this band become,
so daring in their outrages, that they had received
the title of the Brigands of the Prairie.   Indeed, on
more than one occasion they had met the Mexican
troops, and boldly given them battle, until the stolen
herds were driven safely away.   It was to watch
these daring villains, and if possible to bring them
to justice, that the United States soldiers had been
despatched to Tacos, in whose vicinity it was understood the headquarters of the outlaws were, while
it was also a favourite point of theirs for crossing
the river.

Lieutenant Wenie had hardly finished changing his
clothes when an orderly informed him that Major
Curtin, the officer in command of the detachment,
desired to see him.

The lieutenant proceeded at once to the quarters
of the major.

The major, who was seated at a table writing, was
a tall, powerfully-built man, probably fifty years of
age.   His figure showed no sign of decay, and the
iron-grey hair and beard alone told of age.

"Sit down, Lieutenant," he said, indicating a chair.
"You've been out this afternoon."

"Yes; you remember I asked permission," replied
the lieutenant.

"True; so you did.   I had forgotten.   I sent an
order to your quarters about three."

" Anything particular, major ?"

" Well, yes ; there is," the major answered, slowly.

" By the way, did you go up the river as you proposed ?"

" Yes ; I had quite an adventure, too," replied the lieutenant, and then he briefly related how he became fast in the quicksand, and was released by the girl.

" Aha !" cried the major, " that *was* quite an adventure. Was the girl an Amazon of red skin ?"

" Far otherwise, and very pretty !" replied the lieutenant, warmly. " One of the prettiest little oval-faces that my eyes ever looked upon—not so dark in complexion either as most of the Mexican women, but of a hue as though she had been tanned by the sun. Then her hair is as black as jet ; her eyes as dark as her hair—a good full eye with an honest look, and then, in figure she's a little fairy of a woman, with *such* a dainty little hand !"

" Why, lieutenant," cried the major in astonishment, " I should judge you to be in love with the lady."

" So I am," replied Wenie, honestly ; " that's the honest truth ; I *am* in love with her."

" You learned her name ?"

" Yes ; Juanita Torres."

" Ah !" and for a moment the major was silent ; then he said abruptly : " I know her father, Juan Torres, very well. His house is about a mile from here, on the El Paso road—a wealthy man, and one of the largest cattle-raisers in this part of the country."

" You know him !" said Wenie, in surprise.

" Oh yes, very well. Before I entered the arm, I resided in Santa Fe ; I was a trader then ; this Torres also lived in Santa Fe ; he and I were rivals for the hand of the same girl; she was a Mexican, like himself, but preferred me to him, and we married ; my wife had a sister a few years younger than herself ; this sister Torres afterward married."

"Why, major!" exclaimed the lieutenant, "I never knew that you had been married. I never heard you speak of it before."

"Because the subject is somewhat painful; but as you are in love with this man's daughter, it is my duty, as your friend, to let you know what sort of a man you will have to deal with. This Torres, like nearly all his nation, was of a treacherous and revengeful nature ; I do not think that he ever forgave me for marrying Inez—that was my wife's name—and though he had apparently consoled himself for her loss by marrying her sister, yet in his heart I am satisfied he cherished plans of vengeance against me. A year passed, and the world went well with me ; a son was born ; my wife, to my eyes, grew more and more beautiful each day ; I was as happy as man could be, but when my boy was some eight months old a terrible blow fell upon me. The nurse, with the infant, went out one afternoon as usual; the child and nurse never returned. The loss of the infant broke my wife's heart—she sickened and died. This sorrowful event is the reason why you have never heard me speak of my married life. I try to keep my sorrow locked fast in my own breast." And the grim old major bent his head in evident pain.

"And did you not discover the fate of your child ?"

"No, never," the major answered, sadly. "Both nurse and child disappeared as utterly as if the earth had opened and swallowed them up. The search for them was long and fruitless. At last all came to the conclusion that the nurse, with the child, had wandered too far out on the prairie and had fallen a prey to wild beasts."

" And did you, too, come to that conclusion?" asked the lieutenant.

" No."

" No?" cried Wenie, in surprise.

" I believed that the child lived. I believe that the child, now grown to man's estate, is still living. I did not blame the wild beasts of the prairie for the loss of my boy; I ascribed the calamity to a human foe."

" To a human foe?" cried the lieutenant, still more astonished.

" Yes, to a human foe," repeated the major, solemnly. " To one who bore me a secret hatred, a hatred that he did not dare to show openly, but a hatred which he wished me to feel, and so he struck me in my tenderest points—my wife and child; he stole my child, and it killed my wife. Could vengeance go further?"

" And did you not have a suspicion as to who that foe was?" asked Wenie.

" Oh, yes; during the search he was by my side, the most untiring of all—the last man to give up the child as lost, and then he piously said that it was Heaven's will."

" And that man's name?" asked the lieutenant anxiously, for he had a shrewd suspicion as to what the name would be.

" Was Torres—the father of the girl who saved your life, and with whom you are in love," replied the major.

" But had you not any proof that he was guilty?"

" No; if I had, I would have killed him with my own hand," said the soldier, fiercely. " The villain,

if he did commit the deed, covered up his tracks too
well for mortal eye to discover them ; yet in my soul
I felt sure then, and do still feel sure, that it was
his hand that dealt me the terrible blow. After this
occurrence—as you will probably suppose—I had but
little taste for business. I gave up my store, and
devoted myself to discovering traces of my lost boy.
For three years I kept a steady watch upon all the
movements of Juan Torres, but my patience availed
me nothing ; no clue could I discover. Then I gave
my child up as lost, and I sought forgetfulness of my
misery in the bustle of the great eastern cities.
Years passed; the war came, I enlisted at once. I
won my present grade ; and now you know the history of my life. When, at Santa Fe, I was ordered
on this expedition, and I learned that Torres had a
hacienda near here, I thought perhaps fate might
place in my way, after this lapse of years, some clue
to tell me of the fate of my lost boy."

"Major, I hope sincerely that such will be the
case," said the lieutenant, earnestly. "You have my
deepest sympathy."

"I hope so," replied the major. "You see, however, what my opinion is regarding the father of this
girl. By the way, to judge from your description,
this Juanita must be strikingly like my wife, her
mother's sister ; you can judge, therefore, how beautiful my wife must have been when I married her,
and you can also judge how deeply I felt the blow
that tore her from me."

"Yes," replied the lieutenant, and in his own mind
he fully realised how hard it would be for him to
part from the beautiful Juanita, should he succeed
in once winning her.

"And now, to business," said the major. "Have
you any idea why we are detailed for duty here at
Tacos?"

" None in the world," answered the lieutenant.

" You have heard, of course, of the Brigands of the Prairie ?"

" Yes."

" Well, our present occupation here is to hunt down and destroy the famous band of robbers."

" Is it possible !" cried the lieutenant, in glee at the prospect of active service.

" Yes; I have already explained to Lieutenant Williams the object of our expedition. This, of course, must be kept a profound secret, for if these fellows should once guess our design, good-bye to our chance of breaking up the band. From information received at headquarters it is believed that the band have a refuge somewhere near here; it is intimated that some wealthy Mexican in this neighbourhood is one of the leaders of the brigands—not an acting leader, but a planning one."

" But, major, how do you expect to detect these fellows, for they will most certainly keep quiet while the troops are in the neighbourhood ?" asked the lieutenant.

" Very true; but there is a spy among them, who, if the brigands *have* a headquarters near here, will most surely find it out. These fellows will not suspect that we are sent here to operate against them, and will not, probably, change their programme on our account. By the way," said the major, suddenly, " are you going to visit this young lady whose acquaintance you made in such a peculiar manner ?"

" Yes, of course; I again confess to you, major, that I am too deeply interested in her to give her up," said Wenie, candidly.

" It is but natural," replied the major. " I was young myself once; I can understand the feeling; but, Wenie, if you go to the house of Juan Torres. keep your eyes about you."

The lieutenant looked at the major in astonishment. " What do you mean ?"

" Simply that, if there is any man in this neighbourhood who knows anything about the Brigands of the Prairie, I'll bet my commission against a bottle of wine that *Torres is the man*." The major spoke in a tone of conviction.

" I hope not, for her sake ! " cried Wenie.

" Don't despair ; the daughter may not take after the father. I hope, for your sake, she does not," said the major.

And after a few more words the officers parted.

CHAPTER III.
THE GAY CAVALIER.

THE shades of night had descended upon the prairie ; all objects were wrapped in the same gloomy mantle ; the moon — pale mistress of the night – rose late, and her silver beams had not yet fallen upon the broad surface of the green plains.

We will leave Tacos to the darkness and the gloom of the still June night, and take the road leading north, to El Paso ; but, ere we shall have proceeded a mile or so on our way, we shall come to a large hacienda—that is, in Mexican, the house of a landed proprietor who raises cattle—and that hacienda is the home of Juan Torres, the wealthiest man for leagues around, and the father of the pretty Juanita.

The hacienda of Torres was, like nearly all the Mexican houses, a large, square building built of adobe—the sun-burnt brick of Mexico—and in its frowning grimness resembled a fortress more than the peaceful dwelling-place of a cattle-raiser.

The house was a very old one, and around it quite a deal of shrubbery had sprung up, making, as it were, a fruitful oasis in the grassy wilderness.

The entrance to the house faced directly to the road, though a hundred paces from it, and the approach to it was through a little lane fringed with half-grown trees and full-grown bushes.

As we have said, tho night was very dark, and as the windows of the hacienda—Mexican fashion—looked only on the square court-yard in the centre of the building, no rays of light came from the house to illume the darkness that surrounded it.

Yet, in the darkness, close to the house, beneath the shadow of somo little trees, as if seeking concealment more than the inky blackness of the night afforded, stood two persons engaged in earnest conversation – one a man, the other a woman.

The woman was but a slender girl of eighteen, yet lithe and graceful in form as the bending willow ; the tint of the pure oval face was a rich brown, as though the hot prairie sun had kissed her oft and passionately ; her eyes a jet black, eyes full of passion—full of fire ; her hair as dark as the hue of the raven's wing ; her lips, little, pouting, and exquisite in their colour and dewy froshness ; her form, perfection itself—that of a girl just budding into womanhood ; even the coarse garments that she wore could not disguise the matchless beauty of her perfect form, and yet, this beautifnl creature was a peon girl, but one degree removed from a slave !

These peons form a large proportion of tho inhabitants of all the Mexican frontier towns. They are the descendants of the Indians, civilised and tamed by the mission priests—tho free spirit of the savage degraded to the menial offices of the slave. Thus it comes that the peons are the drudges of tho Mexicans. And this lovely girl was ono of that degraded race. Sho was the waiting-maid of Juanita, and by name was called Rita.

And the man that stood by her side, holding secret converse with her, shielded from observation by the inky mantle of the night—who was he? Not a peon, for the whiteness of the features—could we see them in the darkness—and the richness of his attire, would quickly prove that. No, he was a Mexican, and, judging by his garb, a wealthy one, for his embroidered pantaloons are of the finest cloth, his yellow boots of the softest and best of leather, the frilled white shirt that covers his manly chest is made of the finest linen, the jacket is as richly ornamented as the pantaloons, his broad-brimmed sombrero is trimmed with gold lace, and the handsome striped shawl cast carelessly over his left shoulder, has not a superior in price in all the broad lands of Mexico. The face of the young man—for he was young in years, scarcely reaching twenty-five—was a handsome one, save that his full lips had sometimes a peculiar curl, and his dark-grey eyes—almost black in hue—had an uncertain, treacherous glance.

And the name of this young Mexican, who was so forgetful of the dignity of his race as to meet the peon girl Rita, with love on his lips, after nightfall and in the gloom of darkness? He was called Ruy Lara, a nephew of Juan Torres, but hitherto a stranger to the hacienda of that gentleman, for, seven days before, no one of the household, save the master alone, knew that such a person as Ruy Lara existed in the world. Without warning he had made his appearance; Juan Torres received him with open arms—called him his much-loved nephew—and lamented that family reasons had hitherto kept him a stranger to his uncle's hearth and home.

And in the seven days that Ruy Lara had spent at the hacienda of Torres he had done much; he had snown himself to be one of the best and boldest riders that ever crossed back of horse; he had shown that, with the pistol, rifle, or knife, few men were his equal; and he had managed—how, even he himself could not tell—to make his pretty cousin, Juanita' hate him, and her waiting-maid, the even prettier Rita, to adore him. Hence it is that we find him now holding a love tryst with the peon girl.

"Oh, Ruy, and do you really love me?" asked the girl, yielding herself readily to the fond embrace of the young Mexican and holding up her lips to receive his passionate kiss.

"Do I love you, Rita?" he cried, passionately; "you are the light of my heart. Till my eyes fell upon your face I never fancied woman, but now I feel that I am devoted, heart and soul, to you."

"Can I believe you?" asked the girl, striving to see his eyes through the darkness—those mirrors of the soul, that are so hard to hide deceit. But darkness hid the grey orbs from her view, and, had she seen them, they would have proved the truth of his words, for they were full of passionate love.

"Can you believe that the stars shine when your own eyes see them? Can you believe that the waters of the Rio Grande roll onward to the ocean? Can you believe that truth is truth? Then believe in my love."

"But, I am only a poor peon girl," she murmured.

"What of that?" he said. "Love is not measured by station. By heaven, were there no other way to win you, I would strip off this gaudy dress I wear and in a peon's garb work daily in the fields for your sake. Oh, foolish child! will you not believe I love you?"

"Yes, yes, I do believe it," she said softly, clinging to her lover's breast.

"That's right!" he cried, imprinting a kiss upon her full red lips: "but, do you love me?"

"Yes," said the peon girl, softly.

"Better than anyone else?"

"Yes, better than my own life."

"And when I will it, you will fly with me?"

"Fly with you?" she cried, astonished.

"Yes, fly with me," he repeated. "I cannot make you mine here. If you love me you must go with me; you must follow my fortunes, for good or evil, for life or death."

"You are right; I will go with you," she answered. "That will prove that I love you, for if I go with you I shall leave my brother, the Pathfinder, whose love has been all in all to me. Yet for your sake I will leave even him; I will leave the whole world for you."

"You are an angel of a girl," cried the Mexican, "and now I am sure that you love me."

"You shall see that I do," she said, earnestly.

"I shall arrange matters so that within a week or so I can make you mine. I do not think anyone in the hacienda has any suspicions that we care for each other."

"I am afraid my brother has," she replied.

"Ah indeed! What makes you think so?" he asked anxiously.

"I noticed this afternoon that he seemed to be watching us, and that was the reason that I avoided you. My brother has a hot temper, and if he suspected our love and thought you meant me wrong, he would kill you, for he is as fierce in anger as a cougar," said the girl, still clinging to the breast of her lover.

"He is different then from peons generally: they are not given to brave deeds," replied the Mexican.

"My brother is not like a peon," the girl answered. "He has never worked in the fields, but has always

roamed over the prairies. He is called the Pathfinder, for he knows the land for many a league. He
is expert in the use of all weapons, and so brave
that even the Comanches fear him."

"There is no danger," replied Ruy. "I will
arrange your flight so that no one will suspect that
I had a hand in it; and then, far away from this spot,
we will find happiness—happiness such as mortals
seldom enjoy on earth."

"And you will always love me?" asked the girl.

"Always!" he replied, passionately, and sealed the
pledge with a kiss upon the red lips so fondly up-
turned to his.

Then, steps approaching up the little road alarmed
the lovers.

"Someone is coming!" cried the girl.

"Fly to the house, quick!" exclaimed the Mexican.
"I will remain here; the shadows of the trees will
conceal me."

"No! no! If it is my brother, I must meet him.
Go quickly!" cried Rita, and Ruy noiselessly ran
through the darkness to the house.

Rita remained quietly in the shadow of the trees.
Would she be noticed? Useless thought!

The new-comer, whose eyes seemed to have the
cat-like faculty of seeing in the dark, came straight
to her.

"Rita," he said, "what are you doing here?" and
the voice told her that it was her brother, the Pathfinder, who spoke.

"The house was warm; here it is cool," she answered

"Are you alone?" he asked, suspiciously.

"Yes; do you not see that I am?" she said, reading her brother's suspicion in an instant.

"Rita, I have something to say to you," and her
brother's voice had a touch of sternness.

" Well ?" she asked.

" This stranger, Ruy Lara, has his thoughts upon you."

" Do you think so ?" asked Rita, her voice betraying no emotion.

"And you *love him!*"

The darkness concealed the start that the peon girl gave at these words.

" You do not answer," said the brother, after a pause.

" What should I say ?" demanded Rita. " If I deny it, you will not believe me."

" For I know it is the truth. My eyes, that can read the dimmest trail on the prairie and tell where the wolf has passed, are not deceived when the king-wolf is around in human shape. Do you know why Ruy Lara comes here ?" asked the Pathfinder.

" No."

" It is to marry Torres' daughter, Juanita."

" It is impossible," cried Rita.

" It is the truth. Would to Heaven it were not, but it is the truth," said the herdsman, sadly. " She is far too good and pure for such as he. Alas ! alas !"

" What difference does it make to you ?" asked Rita, in wonder. " You are not her keeper !"

" No, not her keeper. She is my keeper. *I* love Juanita myself !" and the stately head of the peon sunk upon his breast as he made the confession.

" What ?" exclaimed Rita, in astonishment. " You, a peon, dare to love the daughter of our master ?"

" Why not ?" returned Manuel. " Do not you, a peon, love the nephew of our master—a man that seven days ago you had never seen—who may be, for aught you know, stained with the blackest of crimes ? Juanita and I have been brought up to-

gether; five years her senior, I have watched over
her like a brother, but, till this man came to woo her,
I did not dream that I loved her. But now I know
that it is so."

" My poor brother !" cried Rita, caressingly passing
her arms around his neck.

" Yes, I am poor," he returned, bitterly ; " poor in
birth and poor in love. But, sister, remember my
warning ; beware of the love of this man ! "

"I shall remember, brother," she said, as together
they proceeded to the hacienda.

Then, like a snake, from beneath the covert of the
bushes, crept a listener—a man who had heard all.
that had passed—a man dressed roughly and poorlyr

" So," he said to himself, " a sort of a triangula,
love affair ! Good ! All's fish that comes to my net.
This may aid me in some way. Aha ! Tio, the Rat
thou art rightly named, and must have had the devil
for a godfather. But now, to enter the enemy's
camp." And with a firm step, the roughly-dressed
fellow approached the door of the hacienda and
knocked loud and lustily.

CHAPTER IV.
THE LEADER OF THE BRIGANDS.

In his private chamber—lighted now by wax-candles
stuck in massive gold candlesticks—sat the owner of
the hacienda, Juan Torres, a man well in years, yet
showing few traces of age. Small and slender was he
in figure; his face was of the true Mexican type,
sallow and thin, lit up by piercing black eyes; the
lips—over which curled a thin moustache, black in
hue like the hair of its owner, but streaked here and
there with silver lines—were thin and closely com-
pressed—lips denoting treachery and low cunning;
his garb was that usually worn by Mexicans of the

better class, for, though the hacienda of Torres was
situated in Texas, yet, like many others on the Texan
frontier, he was, to all intents and purposes, as much
a Mexican as though he lived miles westward from
the Rio Grande.

The other occupant of the chamber was Torres'
nephew, Ruy Lara. Ruy bore but little resemblance
to his uncle; his skin was much fairer; he was much
larger built in person; tho eyes alone betrayed the
relationship.

"Sit down, Ruy," said Torres; "I desire to have
a few words of explanation with you."

"I am completely at your service, uncle," returned
Ruy, carelessly flinging himself into a seat.

"Now, to begin at the beginning, we commence
about the time of the earliest remembrance, which
was when you were about six years old," said Torres,
watching his nephew's face with his cold, glittering
eyes.

"Exactly," responded Ruy, with a look of astonishment at this strange beginning; "though I don't
really see what you want to go quite as far back as
that for."

"Wait and then you will see," said Torres, coolly.
"At the age of six years where were you?"

"Living with on old peon woman, my nurse, near
the city of Mexico, in a miserable little hovel," replied
Ruy, with a shrug of the shoulder, as if the remembrance did not please him.

"That is right," returned Torres; "your history
was an extremely simple one. Your mother, my
sister, married a man who deserted her and her infant child; she died, you were left; you had no
claim on me, for I had disowned my sister for her
marriage. What would have been your probable fate
in this world had I not extended to you a helping

hand?" and the eyes of Torres look searchingly in the face of Ruy as he put the question.

"I should probably have starved," replied Ruy, bluntly.

"Right; the chances are that you would have done so, but I gave you my hand, and you lived; therefore, you owe to me your life; is it not so?" asked Torres.

"Yes, I acknowledge the debt," replied the young man.

"Good. Then, at the age of six, I took charge of your fortunes. I sent you to school till you were ten; then I sent you to the prairie to learn in the school of life. You were an apt scholar. When you were sixteen, few men on the frontier could ride or fight better than you."

"That, I believe, is true," said Ruy, honestly, and without a tinge of boasting. "I have never yet met my master."

"Then, at sixteen, I placed you in another school——"

"Yes," interrupted Ruy; "this time it was a school of cut-throats, thieves, and assassins. Now, uncle, that is what has been a puzzle to me; till the time I was sixteen you acted to me like a father, and then why you should place me in the position that you did, to make me a villain, and put me in peril both here and hereafter, is what I cannot understand."

"Bah! what do you call peril? Being connected with the Brigands of the Prairie? I have been one o them for years; am I any the worse for it?" asked Torres, his shrewd eyes sparkling.

"Well, perhaps not; still, I have an idea that a man is better off to lead an honest life," returned Ruy.

"Honesty!" cried Torres, with a dry laugh;

"honesty in this world is a fable; besides, what chance is there for discovery? For twenty years the Brigands of the Prairie have existed, and they will exist for twenty more. But to proceed: ever since you were sixteen you have been a member of that band; you have distinguished yourself——"

"Yes," interrupted Ruy, dryly; "so much so that my head on the other side of Rio Grande is worth a hundred ounces."

"That shows how dangerous the Mexican Government thinks you. You know that, ten days ago, at our ranche on the Rio Pecos, Miguel Garcia, chief of the Brigands of the Prairie, died."

"Yes, from an accident in the shape of a loaded pistol in the hand of a drunken brigand," observed Ruy.

"Such accidents will happen in bands like ours. Garcia's death leaves us without a chief. You are aware that our band in principle is a republic; the next chief will be elected within a week; forty of our band have the right to vote for that chief, and of the forty votes I control twenty that I can surely count on."

Ruy stared at his uncle in amazement.

"Why, then, that gives you the power to elect the chief that controls our band."

"Exactly," replied Torres, "and I want a chief who will act my will. Garcia was a hot-headed fool, who imagined that he alone had brains; he crossed me once too often; the result, his death."

Ruy made up his mind that, of all the scoundrels he had met during his career—and the number was great—his uncle was certainly the greatest.

"Well, uncle," said Ruy, "I don't exactly understand what this has to do with me."

"Simply that I am about to make you chief of the Brigands of the Prairie," said Torres, calmly.

"What!" Ruy started as if he had received an electric shock. "I chief?"

"Yes; you are devoted to me; you will do my will; you shall be chief of the brigands; I will be the brain of that chief. Is it a bargain?"

"Yes," cried Ruy at once; "I agree."

"Now for another subject," said Torres. "You know it is my purpose to form a union between you and my daughter?"

"Yes; but as the young lady seems to have taken a violent dislike to me, I don't exactly see how you are going to carry out the idea."

"Ruy, you know that I am rich?"

"Yes," replied the young man.

"All I nave will go to my daughter's husband."

"Well, I am perfectly willing, if she is," said Ruy.

"She must be willing!" cried Torres, fiercely. "She has the stubborn spirit of her mother, but I will bend her to my will. She must marry you."

"Good; force is a great persuader. I know she almost hates me," observed Ruy.

"You have not tried to win her love; you have been blindly infatuated with the peon girl Rita."

"The deuce!" cried Ruy to himself; "what sharp eyes that precious old man has!"

"Why do you seek this girl?" asked Torres.

"Well, honestly, I love her," said Ruy.

"Yes, as a child loves a new toy; and, like the child, you would soon tire and throw it away."

"That's extremely possible," said Ruy, coolly; "that has been the case with all my loves before."

"Be careful," said Torres; this girl has a brother, a stout fellow, who will probably call you to account if you wrong his sister."

"I shall act cautiously, rest assured," replied Ruy

"By the way, did yon know that there is a detachment of U nited States soldiers in Tacos?"

"The deuce! no!" cried Ruy, with a start.

"Yes; a full company of cavalry."

"Can they suspect our retreat on the Rio Pecos?" exclaimed Ruy.

"No; there isn't any danger of that being discovered. One of the officers has seen Juanita."

"Well, what of it?" asked Ruy.

"She saved him from the quicksand by the bank of the Rio Grande; he was sinking when she came to his aid. She invited him to call here."

"He won't discover anything."

"Ruy, are you blind?" asked Torres, impatiently. "Juanita is half in love with this officer, whose life she has saved; give them but a few opportunities for meeting, and not all the persuasion and force in this world will make Juanita marry you."

"What is to be done?" asked Ruy.

"As yet nothing. When Juanita told me of this chance-meeting I told her that the visits of this officer here would not be pleasant, and that I should not receive him. I shall instruct the servants when this officer comes to give him such a reception that he will not repeat his visit," said Torres.

"Bravo!" cried Ruy. "Ah, uncle, we shall win the game."

"Yes, but we must play with loaded dice," returned Torres, coolly. "And, to commence at once, tell ono of the servants to send Juanita to me. I shall tell her that she must look upon you as her affianced husband; and, boy, be careful in regard to this peon girl, Rita. Do as you will with her, but mask it from the world."

And with this one injunction in his ears, Ruy withdrew.

"Strange how I love that boy," the old man murmured to himself after Ruy had left the apartment. "I love him far better than I do my own girl; it is for *her* sake, I suppose, for heaven knows I hated the father with all my heart."

The entrance of Juanita put an end to his meditations.

" You wished to see me, father," she said, and it was plainly evident from her manner that there was but little love between the father and daughter.

" Yes, my child," said Torres, looking intently in his daughter's face. "You have grown to womanhood; it is time to think of a husband for you."

Juanita trembled at this beginning. She had understood fully the meaning of the glances that Ruy Lara had bestowed upon her; and in her heart sho hated him. Why, she could not tell, for he never offended her in any way, but some secret instinct warned her against him.

" How do you like my nephew, Ruy Lara?" questioned her father, when he found that she did not speak.

"I do not like him," answered Juanita, honestly.

"I am sorry for that, for he is to be your future husband," returned the father.

" Whether I love him or no?" asked Juanita, in amazement.

" You are a foolish child; you do not know the meaning of the word love!" cried Torres, testily.

" I know that I can never love my cousin!" exclaimed Juanita, passionately. "I know that I hate him."

" Hate him!" cried her father. "Why do you hate him?"

" I do not know," replied Juanita; " but his very presence is distasteful to me."

"Do you love anyone else?" questioned Torres, quietly.

A burning blush spread over Juanita's cheeks and forehead at the question.

"No, no," she murmured; "whom should I love?"

"How can I tell?" said Torres, coldly. "Young ladies of your age sometimes take strange fancies into their heads. But, fancy or no fancy, you may consider your fate settled. Within a week you will be married to your cousin Ruy."

"Then you do not care whether I love him or do not love him?" asked Juanita, in amazement.

"No," replied Torres, shortly.

"And does he care as little for my feelings toward him?" demanded the girl.

"He loves you, and will marry you; let that suffice," said Torres, determinedly.

"Father, hear me," exclaimed Juanita—all the strength of her woman's nature aroused. "I do not love Ruy Lara, and of my own free will I shall never marry him."

"You are a foolish child," returned the father. "Go to your room; you will think better of this. Time will convince you that you had best submit and do my bidding."

"Never, father!" cried Juanita, as she left the apartment.

CHAPTER V.
THE MEETING ON THE PRAIRIE.

THE next morning came clear and beautiful. After breakfast, Ruy saw in the courtyard a man whose face seemed strangely familiar to him. The man was evidently a stranger; his dress was poor and well worn; in size he was about the medium height—in face a Mexican. Ruy called Torres' attention to the man, and asked who he was.

" Oh, a poor devil who came along last night, beg-ging for work," answered Torres, " and as, by his own account, he is a good herdsman, I engaged him."

" It is strange how familiar his face is to me," said Ruy, slowly, as if trying to place the features in his memory.

" It is a common face," said Torres. " It is evident that the poor devil has suffered from want in the past." And so the subject of the stranger, who was no other than the listener in the bushes of the pre-ceding evening, who had called himself Tio, the Rat, was dismissed.

After breakfast, Juanita mounted her horse—the cream-coloured mustang—and rode off. At first she rode directly north, toward El Passo, then, fairly out of sight of the hacienda, she made a wide circuit round to the south and rode toward Tacos.

What object had Juanita in this early ride? She could hardly have told herself, save that in her heart she had a secret hope that she might meet the young officer whose life she had saved, and whose image since that moment had ever been before her.

Riding briskly on, the town of Tacos soon rose be-fore her, and then, to her joy, galloping up the road from the town, she saw the young lieutenant, who, if truth be told, had ridden forth that morning in hopes of meeting with the fair Mexican girl.

The delight at the meeting then was mutual.

" You are in the saddle early," said the lieutenant, as they met.

" Yes," she replied, striving to conceal the joy which sparkled in her eyes. " I love to ride."

" If you will accept my escort, I shall be pleased to accompany you," said the officer.

" I shall be delighted," replied the girl, truthfully.

So, side by side, the lovers—for such, in truth,

C

they were in heart, although their lips had never declared it—rode along. They turned their conrse toward the rivor, and, reaching it, rode along parallel with the Rio Grande.

"Pardon me," said Wenie, as he noticed the slight cloud upon the face of his fair companion, "but you do not look well this morning—you seem sad; are you ill?"

"No," Juanita replied, with a half-smile; "but," and she looked earnestly at the young officer to note the effect of her words, "I am going to be married."

"Married!" cried the lieutenant, in despair; and his face showed plainly how keen was the blow.

"Yes," continued Juanita, delighted with what she saw in the face of her companion, "married to a man I do not and cannot love."

"Why, then, do you marry him?"

"It is my father's will; he forces me to it."

"Surely, your father should consult your happiness before proceeding on a step like this," said the lieutenant, in amazement.

Juanita shook her head sadly.

"My father cares very little for aught but his own pleasure. He intends to force me to marry, whether I will or no."

"By heaven!" cried Wenie, hotly, "he is not worthy of the name of father. Is there no escape for you?"

"I can see none," replied Juanita. "In seven days I am to be married."

For a moment Wenie was silent; busy thoughts were in his mind. Should he stand tamely by and see this beautiful girl sacrificed, and she, too, the only girl that he felt he ever had really loved—sacrificed to a man she did not love? No, he would speak, and win or lose all.

"Juanita," he said, and his strong manly voice trembled as he spoke, "I have only known you for a few hours, but it seems to me as if years had passed since we first met. You are the first girl I have ever seen that I felt I could love with my whole heart. I should have kept this a secret, but what you have told me makes me speak. Juanita, I love you, and I cannot be distasteful to you. Can you love me a little?"

The two horses had stopped, the riders were side by side.

"No, not a little," replied the blushing girl; "but, like you, with all my heart."

Overjoyed, he clasped her gently in his arms; their lips met in the pure and holy kiss that true love gives to true love.

"Mine! for ever mine!" cried the lieutenant, as he looked full into the dark eyes that now gazed so lovingly into his.

"Yes, for ever and for ever," replied Juanita.

"But your father will never consent to our marriage," said the lieutenant.

"No, never."

"Will you go with me, then, and become mine despite his wishes?" asked Wenic anxiously.

"Yes, to the end of the world. My father does not treat me as a daughter; why, then, should I give that obedience which should be his due?"

"There is a priest in the village; he shall marry us, and once you are mine, I defy all human power to take you from me. Can you leave your father's hacienda to-morrow about this time without exciting suspicion?"

"Yes," answered the girl.

"I will meet you here, and in the interval I will see the priest and prepare all things for the cere-

mony. We must lose no time, for if your father or
this favoured rival of mine—to whom perforce they
intend to marry you—should discover our love, they
hay devise some plan to separate us. Do you consent to this hasty union? "

· " Yes," answered Juanita, trustfully giving her
hand to her lover; "your will is my will; whatever
you say, I will do. But now let us part, that we may
not be seen together, and our plot be suspected."

" Farewell, then, beloved," cried the lieutenant;
"remember to-morrow."

" I shall not forget ! " exclaimed the girl, gazing
with those eyes so full of love into the face of her
lover.

A warm pressure of the hands and they parted;
the lieutenant taking the road to the village, Juanita
that which led northward to her father's house.

Hardly had she faced her horse about and commenced her homeward journey, when, to her dismay,
she perceived her cousin, Ruy Lara, on horseback.
approaching rapidly.

" Could he have seen me part with the lieutenant ? "
was the question that mentally passed through her
mind, and as Ruy galloped up she cast a searching
glance at his features, trying to read his mind in his
face. The attempt was fruitless, though, for Ruy's
face wore the usual half-sneering smile common
to it.

" Taking a gallop, my fair cousin ? " he said smil-
ingly, as he halted his horse before her.

" Yes," she replied curtly, drawing her horse off to
the left, as if to pass him; but, with a quick movement, he wheeled his horse around, and rode beside
her.

" Homeward now, Juanita ? " he asked.

" Yes," she answered.

She took but little pains to conceal her dislike.

"I'll keep you company, then," he replied. "By the way," he said abruptly, as they rode along, "you have had an escort this morning, I presume. Was that not one of the officers of the troops stationed in Tacos, that I saw you parting with just now?"

Juanita felt that it would be useless to attempt to disguise the truth.

"Yes," she answered, "it was."

"Was it the same officer whose life you saved yesterday, in the quicksand?" he said carelessly. "Lieutenant—by the way, what is his name?"

"Wenie," she answered, and then the next instant could have bitten off her tongue for speaking, for her quick eye noted the look of exultation that flashed over Ruy's face when he learned the name of his rival.

"Juanita, do you know I've half a mind to be jealous?" he said slowly. "To see my affianced wife riding alone with a dashing young officer, and he, too, but the acquaintance of a day, is not very pleasant."

"Indeed!" and Juanita's lip curled in scorn; "am I your affianced wife? I was not aware that you had done me the honour to ask me for my hand."

The coolness of the girl disconcerted the redoubtable Ruy, who was certainly not troubled with bashfulness.

"Your father arranged the whole affair," he replied, "and I thought, of course, that it included your consent; but, to make the matter fully understood, Juanita, I love you, and ask you to be my wife."

"Senor, I am sorry; but I do not return your passion," said the girl, coldly, "and I must decline your offer."

"It is your father's will!" exclaimed Ruy.

"You will find that my father's will does not bind my hand!" exclaimed Juanita, indignantly, while the hot blood mounted into her cheeks.

"You refuse me then ?" asked Ruy.

"Yes," replied the girl, firmly, "I do !"

"Perhaps you are in love with somebody else," returned Ruy, sneeringly—"perhaps with this North American officer—this cursed *gringo*! Let him beware how he crosses my path, for, if he does, not all the fiends below can save him from my vengeance."

"Threatened men live long, senor; possibly the life of this American will not be shortened by your words," replied Juanita, in scorn.

"We shall see!" cried the Mexican, hotly; "but his wife you never will be."

"Your wife I never will be!" returned Juanita, all the fire of her nature aroused.

"That remains to be proved," replied Ruy; "but for this officer, I will take care of him."

Juanita understood the covert threat, but she had little fear; she felt sure that her lover was more than a match for Ruy Lara.

"I shall tell your father of this stolen interview," continued Ruy.

"Tell what you please. I judge from what little I have seen of you that it is like your nature to play the spy; but the interview was not, as you say, a 'stolen' one. I met the officer, by chance, openly on the prairie. I did not dream that my steps were watched, or that my cousin would descend to play the spy upon my actions." The tone of the girl was full of bitterness, and the young Mexican felt keenly the sting of her words.

By this time, they had reached the hacienda. Both dismounted, gave their horses to the charge of the servants and entered the house. Juanita proceeded at once to her chamber, while Ruy sought Senor Torres.

"Well?" questioned Torres, when Ruy entered his room, for he saw plainly, by his angry look, that something had happened.

"Juanita has been riding with this officer—curse him!—upon the prairie," cried Ruy.

"Ah!" and the brows of the old Mexican grew dark with anger; "how do you know?"

"I saw them part on the road near Tacos, and, judging from the time that Juanita left the house this morning, they must have been together two hours at least."

"That is bad," said Torres, musingly. Can this officer be in love with her?"

"Nothing more natural," returned Ruy. "She saved his life. At all events, I am sure of one thing, she is in love with him."

Torres started, and his face plainly showed his anger at this intelligence.

"What is to be done with this headstrong girl?" cried the father.

"Send her away until we can arrange everything for the marriage—send her to our rancho, on the Rio Pecos. Let her go there at night; be kept closely housed after she is there, and she will not suspect the character of the place."

"The plan is good!" cried Torres; "it shall be carried out. She shall depart this very night. This soldier shall be thrown completely off the track."

"Do not fear him," said Ruy, and a peculiar expression appeared on his face. "I shall see him this afternoon; he has come between me and my purposes; he is in danger."

"Be careful; remember he has many at his back."

"My horse is swift; I can easily escape; no one

in the village knows me; besides, I shall leave here to-night."

Ruy left the father to his reflections, which were not altogether pleasant, and went to his own apartment. There he examined the charges in his pistols, tried the point of his knife, and made all preparations as if for a deadly encounter.

CHAPTER VI
A SOLDIER'S WAY.

THE hour of two in the afternoon found Ruy Lara in the saddle, and riding rapidly toward Tacos. He had determined to execute speedy and certain vengeance upon the young officer who had dared to come between him and the beautiful Juanita.

Tacos was not without that usual adjunct to civilisation, a little drinking-house; and to this Ruy directed his way.

The house was a little one-storey structure, built of adobe, but not in the usual Mexican fashion of a square with a courtyard in the centre, for the windows looked directly upon the street.

Ruy's keen eye noted the surroundings of the house as he approached. He dismounted and entered; his well-trained beast remained quietly where he had been left.

The little room that Ruy entered was deserted. He seated himself by a little table close to the window and called loudly for the host.

The keeper of the house, an oily little Mexican, came bustling into the room.

"Welcome, señor," he cried; "what will the senor be pleased to have?"

"Aguardiente" (a Mexican liquor), said Ruy, "and can you find a messenger to carry a message to an officer of the garrison here?"

"Yes, senor," replied the host; "I'll bring him to you."

The host disappeared, but returned in a moment, bringing the liquor, and behind him another Mexican.

"This is the man, senor; he will go," said the host.

Ruy looked at the Mexican, and to his astonishment saw that it was the same fellow whose face had attracted his attention in the courtyard of the hacienda that morning. It was indeed Tio the Rat.

After placing the liquor upon the table, the host discreetly withdrew.

"You are in the household of Senor Torres?" asked Ruy.

"Yes, senor," replied the other with a grin.

"What brings you here?"

"I'm fond of liquor."

The answer was sufficient.

"Do you know me?" asked Ruy.

"That depends upon circumstances," returned Tio, with another grin.

"You are a sensible fellow," said Ruy, "and, at the present time, I am an utter stranger to you: you never saw me before; you understand?"

"Yes, senor," replied Tio.

"And if, in an hour or so, you are questioned as to who or what I am?"

"I shall know nothing!" cried the vagabond Mexican, who formed such a contrast to the other.

"Exactly! I see that you understand me; you shall not lose anything by it," said Ruy. "Now, will you bear a message from me to Lieutenant Wenie, one of the United States officers here?"

"Yes, senor,"

" Say to him that a gentleman desires to see him here on particular business."

" Yes, senor ; I'll fly at once," and the Mexican departed on his errand.

" Aha !" said Tio to himself, as he walked toward the quarters of the soldiers ; " what does Ruy Lara want with the lieutenant ?   I must know."

Ruy, in the meanwhile, drank a little of the potent liquor, loosened the pistols in his belt, and saw that his knife played freely in its scabbard.

Within ten minutes Ruy saw a manly form, decked in the blue of Uncle Sam, pass the window, and in a second more Lieutenant Wenie entered the room.

Ruy had chosen a position with his back to the window.

" You sent a message to me, sir ?" said Wenie, addressing Ruy, the only occupant of the room.

When Wenie had received the message that a Mexican gentleman desired to speak with him, his first thought was that it must be the father of Juanita, who had, by some means, discovered the secret of his daughter's love.   He was surprised then, when he found that it was a young man about his own age who awaited him.

" Yes, senor," replied Ruy, in answer to the officer's question, " I had that honour.   Be seated, senor," he said, motioning to a chair on the opposite side of the table.   The lieutenant sat down.

The table was between the two men, the window right at Ruy's back.

" Now, sir, your business with me ? " asked Wenie, unable to guess why the Mexican should wish a private interview with him.

" You are acquainted with a lady called Juanita Torres ?"

In a moment the truth flashed upon the young officer's mind : the man before him was his rival.

"Yes," he answered ; "I am."

"You are in love with this lady."

"I am too much of a gentleman to dispute your word," returned Wenie, bowing with mock politeness. A red spot gathered in the cheeks of the Mexican at this answer.

"I suppose you are aware that the senorita is engaged to be married?" said Ruy, striving to preserve his coolness.

"How should I be aware of the fact ?" questioned Wenie, blandly.

"Possibly the lady herself may have informed you."

"Possibly," returned the lieutenant.

"Has she not told you?" said Ruy.

"Ah, excuse me," replied Wenie, with formal politeness; "you put a direct question; you really must excuse my answering it."

"In six days the lady is to be married," said the Mexican, feeling that he was getting angry.

"Indeed!" cried the lieutenant, coolly. "Whom to? Are you to be the happy man?"

"That matters not," replied Ruy, shortly, feeling that he was no match in coolness for the American.

"As you say, it matters not," said Wenie. "Only I was about to congratulate you if you were to be the happy bridegroom."

The Mexican felt that there was bitter mockery in the words so lightly spoken, and the blood began to leap fiercely in his veins.

"Senor, you must give up all thoughts of Senorita Torres," he cried.

"*Must!*" returned the lieutenant, coolly. "That is a word foreign to me. But, senor, do you not think

that you are proceeding rather rashly? You come
to me and say that I must give up all thoughts of a
lady that, perhaps, I never have thought of—at least,
you have no proof that I have indulged any expecta-
tions in that direction."

The lieutenant was skilfully leading the Mexican
on, to see if he really had discovered anything.

" Enough that we have a suspicion which, in our
minds, is as strong as certainty,' replied Ruy, his
hand seeking the handle of his pistol - the movement concealed from the eyes of the lieutenant by
the table.

" We !" said the lieutenant, laying a peculiar stress
upon the word ; "and who—if I may be so bold as
to ask the question—does we consist of ?"

" Her father and myself," replied Ruy.

" Ah, now I am sure of it !" cried Wenie. " You
are the gentleman to whom in six days she is to be
wedded. By-the-way, I haven't had the pleasure of
learning your name yet."

" My name does not concern you."

" Oh, yes, it does," replied the lieutenant ; "for I
have an idea that you and I will meet hereafter."

" I think not," said Ruy, grimly, clutching the butt
of his pistol firmly as he spoke. " But you have not
answered my question," he continued. " Will you
resign all thoughts of the lady ?"

" First prove to me that I have thoughts of her ;
then I'll tell you whether I'll resign them or not,"
said the lieutenant, jocosely.

" You are jesting with me !" cried Ruy, fiercely.

" Never was more serious in the whole course of
my life," returned the soldier.

" You will find that this is no laughing matter !"
exclaimed the Mexican, thoroughly angry, and only
waiting for a favourable opportunity to put his plan
in execution.

"Laughing matter?" said Wenie, with a peculiar look—a look that boded danger to the Mexican; "oh, no! you will find before we are through that I am as much in earnest as you are."

"If you do not give up the senorita, force may be used?" cried Ruy, in a tone of menace.

"Force!" repeated Wenie; "the very thought that has been in my mind for the last five minutes, and I've been thinking whether to throw you through the door or through the window," said Wenie, in his quiet way. "You need a lesson, and I think I'll give you one."

"What! you give me a lesson, dog!" cried Ruy, drawing his pistol from beneath the cover of the table.

This epithet had hardly passed his lips, ere the firm hand of the American had dashed the vessel of liquor full in his face. Half-blinded with the drench, Ruy sprung to his feet, leveled his pistol full at the breast of the young officer, and fired; but the movements of Wenie were fully as quick as those of his opponent. Springing to one side, he avoided the shot, and before the Mexican could lower his hand, with a powerful blow, given with all the strength of the muscular arm of the American, he struck Ruy in the neck, right on the jugular vein. Through the open window went the Mexican, stunned and senseless.

"Well, he did go through the window, after all," said Wenie, quietly to himself, as he looked on his helpless foe.

The host, alarmed by the shot, rushed into the room, followed by the Mexican, Tio, who, from the doorway, had watched the scene.

"May the Virgin save us!" cried the host, as his eyes fell upon the senseless form of the Mexican extended on the ground outside; "the man is dead!"

"No, he's worth a dozen dead men," replied the officer. "Bathe his head; he'll soon come to."

And, giving this advice, Wonie departed.

"Bring some liquor!" cried Tio; "but first, help me to bring him in. The devil of an American must have an arm and fist of iron."

Together the host and Tio brought the senseless man into the house.

After repeated applications of liquor to his temples, Ruy slowly revived.

"Ah! my head!" were Ruy's first words.

"Santa Maria!" cried Tio, "a horse couldn't have kicked harder;" and he lost himself in admiration of the deftly-given blow.

Soon Ruy managed to stand upon his feet and comprehend what had passed. For the first time in his life he had met his master. Terrible was the oath of vengeance that he swore.

Weak, and with his head swimming from the effects of the terrible buffet, Ruy mounted his horse, and, attended by Tio, on a patient little mule, took the road homeward. But one thought was in his mind—vengeance!

CHAPTER VII.
THE FLIGHT BY NIGHT.

On the road to the hacienda, Ruy arranged his plans. First, Juanita must be removed from the neighbourhood of Tacos—removed from all chance of ever again seeing the young lieutenant who had given him such a terrible lesson. Second, Rita, the peon girl, must become his, and, in order to effect that, she, too, must be removed from the hacienda—removed from the watchful care of her brother, Manuel, the herdsman. The ranche of the brigands by the Rio Pecos offered a secure retreat. Isolated from the world, Rita once there, there was but little danger of her being discovered. Then, too, there were brigands enough there to hold the ranche against a host, should it, by any fatal chance, be discovered. But who was to convey Rita there? She must have, as an escort across the prairie, one that he could trust. Ruy's eyes fell upon Tio, the apparently half-starved vagabond, riding demurely behind him. And as Ruy looked upon him, again he felt sure that he had seen his face before.

" What is your name? " Ruy asked suddenly.

" Tio," answered the humble follower.

" Tio ! "

" Yes, senor ; by some of my old friends in Mexico I was called Tio the Rat."

" Tio the Rat? " repeated Ruy ! " a strange name! Why did they call you that? "

" Because, I suppose, I possessed the rat-like faculty of living upon almost nothing, and getting it without paying for it," responded the Mexican, with one of his peculiar grins.

" Have I not seen you before, somewhere? " asked Ruy.

A peculiar expression passed across the face of Tio, unnoticed, however, by his companion.

" Yes, senor," he answered.

" In Mexico ? "

" Yes, senor."

" Where ? "

" Does the senor remember a certain New Year's night in the prison in the city of Mexico ? " asked the vagabond.

" Yes, 'twas on that night that I escaped from it; you then must know who I am ? " said Ruy.

" Yes. senor ; one of the leaders of the Brigands of the Prairie. I remembered your face the instant I saw it. I escaped from the prison with you that night."

"I remember now," cried Ruy; "but you were dressed then like a gentleman, and not in wretched rags like these."

"Ah, senor!" cried Tio with a sigh, "Fortune smiled upon me then. Since that time she has frowned upon me."

"Well, since you know our secret, join us; become a Brigand of the Prairie; what say you?" asked Ruy.

"I shall be delighted, senor," responded the other.

"A brave future is in store for you," said Ruy. and now you can do me a service."

"Command me, senor," cried Tio quickly.

"Are you accustomed to the prairie? Can you find your way by night, with no other guide than the stars?"

"Yes, senor," replied the other readily.

"Do you know in what direction the Rio Pecos runs?"

"Yes, senor! it is to the east of us, almost parallel with the Rio Grande."

"Right. Now the service I wish you to do is this: there is a lady in yonder hacienda whom I wish you to conduct to a ranche on the Rio Pecos; the ranche is about a hundred and fifty miles from here. I have a rude map at home by which I can show you the exact position of the place. Do you think you can conduct the lady there?"

"Oh, yes, senor; without a doubt!" cried Tio, and he could hardly conceal his exulation, for he understood fully that this lonely ranche on the Rio Pecos was the headquarters of the Prairie Brigands! Tio the Rat had a strong desire to penetrate to that stronghold.

Reaching the hacienda, Ruy, after warning Tio to keep his tongue between his teeth regarding the expedition on foot, sought Senor Torres.

Eagerly the old Mexican questioned him concerning the young officer.

"I have not been able to accomplish anything," was Ruy's truthful reply.

"Juanita must be got out of his way to-night," said Torres thoughtfully.

"Have you thought of a plan?" asked Ruy.

"Yes; I shall tell my daughter to prepare for a journey to Santa Fe, and start away the moment the shades of night close over the prairie. That report spread among the household will put this officer on the wrong track, if he misses the girl and makes inquiries after her. You must depart at once for the ranche; reaching it, select ten or fifteen men and return to escort us across the prairie."

"Where shall I meet you?" asked Ruy.

"At the old ruined ranche, twenty miles from here, on the El Paso road. When I reach it to-night I will halt, wait for your arrival, then send back my people; they, of course, will think that we have kept straight on for El Paso."

"Excellent!" cried Ruy. "This North American will be thrown completely off the trail; but if he should happen to have a mountain-man in his company—one used to trailing—he might be able to follow us."

"There is little danger of that," said Torres. "These are regular troops, and the mountain-men, used to the free life of the prairie, are not apt to exchange it for the dog's life of the common soldier."

"You will wait at the old ranch till I come, then?" said Ruy.

"Yos," replied Torres. "Make a detour when you approach, so as to come from the north—the El Paso way. It is our people that we must deceive; they must think that we are going to Santa Fe."

"I'll to horse at once and set out!" cried Ruy, and forthwith he left the room. He did not go to the stables, however; but, proceeding cautiously, he entered a small room adjoining that of Juanita—the room of the peon girl, Rita.

"Where is your mistress?" he asked, cautiously.

"She is sleeping," replied the girl.

"Good; we are not likely to be disturbed, then. Rita, are you prepared to fly to-night?"

"To-night!" exclaimed the girl, in surprise.

"Yes, to-night," repeated Ruy. "I am about to set forth now; that will remove all suspicion that I have anything to do with your flight."

"But am I to go alone?" asked Rita, in wonder.

"No; of course not," replied Ruy. "Have you noticed the stranger that came yesterday—the common-looking fellow in the garb of a herdsman?"

"Yes," answered the girl, "you mean Tio?"

"I see you know his name; he is the one I mean. At nightfall he will be waiting with two horses outside the hacienda, just beyond the spot where we held our last meeting. You will go to him. Mount one of the horses; he will act as your guide and protector; you will fly—fly, to finally find shelter in my arms."

"Ah, how happy!" murmured the girl.

"You will do this?" he asked.

"Yes."

"Be sure you are not observed." Then pressing a farewell kiss upon her red lips he left her.

On his way to the stables he met Tio. To him he explained the plan of operations, pointed out the two horses to use, ordered his own horse to be saddled, and then, with Tio, returned to the house. In his room he gave the herdsman a rudely-drawn map, and pointed out the route that he must follow.

He declared that he could find the road blindfold.

Then, satisfied that everything would progress favourably, Ruy swung himself into the saddle and galloped off, bending his course apparently for El Paso.

Torres summoned his daughter. Upon her appearance he informed her that she must prepare to set out at night for Santa Fe.

The words struck a chill to the poor girl's heart. Resistance to her father's command she knew was useless. And then, Juanita thought of the despair that would come upon her lover when, in the morning, he sought out the meeting-place by the flowing Rio Grande, and she came not. Then the thought flashed through her mind, could she not convey the news to her lover that she had been hurried off to Santa Fe? Yes, she could do that, and he might follow and save her.

Briefly Juanita responded to her father, and said that at nightfall she would be ready.

Once in her own room Juanita puzzled her brain how to convey the news to her lover. Then she suddenly thought of Rita, her waiting-maid, and of her brother Manuel, the herdsman. If they would, they could aid her. Yet she felt a reluctance to confess her love to her waiting-maid, for, of course, Rita would suspect the truth, but, for her lover's sake, she resolved to brave all.

Opening the door that led to her waiting-maid's room, she called her. Rita came instantly.

" Rita," said Juanita, a slight blush beginning to bloom upon her cheeks, " I wish you would do me a service."

" Senorita has only to command," replied the peon girl, simply.

"I am going away to night—going to Sant~ F~.
There is someone in Tacos"—and Juanita hesitated
slightly—"that I wish to inform of my departure.
I wish to send a note, and neither my father nor my
cousin must know of it."

It was all plain to the shrewd eyes of the peon
girl: her mistress had a lover in Tacos; it was that
lover that she wished to warn. The heart of Rita
beat for joy; if Juanita loved someone in Tacos, she
did not then love Ruy Lara, and the peon girl felt
that the young Mexican was all her own. Little did
Juanita realise the powerful ally she would have in
Rita, in all schemes the object of which was to unite
her and her lover.

"Do not fear, senorita!" cried Rita; "I will speak
to my brother and he will take your letter safely, and
no one will know of it."

Then suddenly to the mind of the peon girl came
the thought of her brother's confession of his helpless love for his master's daughter. Would he then
take the letter that might be the means of bringing
her to another's arms? No! no! Rita truly felt
that her brother's interest in keeping back the letter
was fully as great as hers to have it delivered.
What, then, was to be done? Suddenly she thought
of the Mexican who was to act as her guide and escort her in that night's flight; *he* would take it—
would imagine that it was her own message, for she
need not mention her mistress's name. Yes, she felt
that plan would do.

Meanwhile, Juanita, at the little table, had been
writing her note—the first note of love in all her life.
It began—

"MY OWN DEAR PHILIP — I have just been told
by my father that I must go at once to Santa Fe.
We start at nightfall. I do not know the meaning of

this strange journey. I think, though, that in some way my father has learned of our love, and it is done to separate us. Sometimes, too, I think that we are not going to Santa Fe, but that I have been told that was my destination so that, if I contrived to communicate with you, it might deceive you, and prevent you from following me. Believe me, Philip, I do not go of my own free will, but because I am forced to. I shall never ceased to love you as long as I live, and will be faithful to you for ever and for ever. Do not give me up, but follow and rescue me from the hands of my cruel relatives.

" Your JUANITA."

The little note was sealed and then addressed, " Lieutenant Wenie." Rita, with the note, hastened to find Tio. That worthy readily agreed to take it, and in an hour afterward Tio was in Tacos. Unfortunately, Wenic, with a squad of men, had gone down the river after some stray horses, and so it happened that he did not receive the note till near ten. Bitterly he deplored the ill-luck that gave his opponents such a start.

At nightfall precisely, Senor Torres, his daughter, and a large escort set out. Almost at the same time, too, Rita and Tio were galloping across the prairie eastward.

Major Curtin sat up late that night, carefully examining a paper spread out on the table before him. This paper was a rude map; on it was traced the course of the Rio Grande and the Rio Pecos. The map was exactly like the one that Ruy Lara had given to Tio the Rat to guide him across the prairie to the ranche of the brigands.

CHAPTER VIII.

THE PATHFINDER ON THE TRAIL.

TORRES and his party reached the old ranche. There they halted till the next day, when they were joined by Ruy and some fifteen stalwart fellows armed to the teeth.

Ruy explained that the Comanche Indians were on the war-path, and he had engaged his escort in El Paso; so those that came with Torres were sent back to the hacienda, and he and his daughter proceeded on their way with the escort headed by Ruy.

The Pathfinder, who was one of those who had accompanied Torres as far as the old ranche, when he returned to the hacienda was astonished to learn that his sister was not there. Those who had remained behind had noticed her absence, but had thought that she had accompanied her young mistress.

The peon felt at once that his worst fears in regard to his sister had been realised. Yet, whither had she gone? That he could not guess. Had he not seen Ruy Lara at the head of the escort with Torres, he would have instantly have suspected that she had fled to join him; and then the thought flashed into the mind of the peon, might it not be so now? Possibly Lara had provided some retreat for his sister, where, at his leisure, he might visit her. The thought was madness to the young herdsman. He instantly resolved to learn the truth, to trail the flying girl to her refuge; but, how had she gone? and whom had she gone with? for it was plainly evident o Manuel that she had fled not alone.

Then Manuel looked through the household to see who was missing; all were there save the stranger who had come but recently and who had said he was called " Tio the Rat."

It was plain, then, to the Pathfinder. This man was a tool of Ruy Lara, and he instantly concluded that it was all a pre-arranged plan—the entrance of Tio into the hacienda of Torres and the flight of his sister.

"But they cannot have flown away!" cried Manuel to himself. "Their horses must have left their hoof-prints on the prairie. I'll track them as the wolf tracks the wounded deer, and, like the bloodhound, I'll die on the trail, but I'll run the game to earth."

Brought up from his earliest infancy on the prairie, possessing the Indian gift of marvellous ear and eye—which even the deadening influence of the half-civilisation that he had passed through had not tampered with—the Pathfinder could follow a trail with the unerring skill of a Comanche.

Burning, then, with the desire for vengeance, the brother proceeded to his task of mingled love and hate.

The prairie just around the hacienda had been trampled over by so many steeds—the horses of the cavalcade—that to find a clue to the presence of the two fugitives was quite out of the question. So he went a thousand good yards from the house; then he commenced to trace a circle around it, carefully examining the soft green sward as he went. Not a blade of grass—not a wind-blown leaf from the shrubbery that surrounded the hacienda escaped his attention.

The Pathfinder had completed a quarter of the circle, when, suddenly, he stopped; his keen eye had caught sight of hoof-prints. Closely he examined them; ten minutes' careful inspection of the trail convinced him that it was the trail he sought.

The herdsman returned to the hacienda, took his

rifle, a supply of ammunition, his horse from the
stable, and then set out upon the prairie trail.

Once out where the grass had not been trampled,
Manuel followed the trail easily,

On pressed the herdsman, till the shades of night
came and forced him to relinquish the chase.
Manuel slept that night beside the trail.

The morning sun found the herdsman again upon
the track, and, ere that sun shone at mid-day over
the prairie, the trail had struck the wooded banks of
the Rio Pecos and had turned northward, following
upward the course of the stream.

Manuel proceeded with caution; he felt that he
was on the eve of a discovery. A sudden turn of
the stream brought to his view a large ranche; the
house built of hewn timber and surrounded by a
heavy stockade fence. Evidently the place had
been built to stand a siege.

A little log-house on the outside of the stockade
and near the bank of the river attracted Manuel's
attention, nestled as it was down among the trees
that grew on the bank of the stream, yet it seemed
to shun observation.

The Pathfinder concealed his horse carefully in the
timber, and then, on foot, taking advantage of the
trees and shrubbery to shield him from observation,
scouted in toward the little lone house. He soon
gained a position which commanded a full view of
the hut door. Hardly had he gained his position,
when, from the door of the stockade, came Ruy
Lara, and advanced toward the hut. Every muscle
in the body of the peon thrilled as, from his covert
unseen, he looked upon the face of the man who he
felt convinced had decoyed away his sister. His
hand sought the rifle ; the life of Ruy Lara would
have been worth but little had the steady arm of the

peon levelled the long piece; but a second thought restrained him; so he watched and waited.

As Ruy Lara approached the house, a man with a gun in his hand rose from the bushes near it—the man was Tio, who had apparently been on guard

"Has anyone attempted to approach the house, Tio?" asked Ruy.

"No, senor," replied Tio.

"You are tired of watching, I suppose?"

"Yes, senor, I haven't got over the effects of tha night's ride yet."

"What is the girl doing?"

How the brother's heart beat when he heard Ruy ask the question! for, from his hiding-place, he could both see and hear—hear every word distinctly. He had little doubt that the girl referred to was Rita.

"She was asleep on the bed, senor, the last time I looked in," responded Tio.

"You need not watch longer," said Ruy. "Go ana refresh yourself."

Tio did not wait for a second bidding, but hurried at once toward the ranche.

Ruy, with a careless glance around, entered the little house, and the door closed behind him.

For full five minutes Manuel waited; then, unable longer to endure the suspense, he determined to satisfy his mind as to whether his sister was in the house or not, whatever might be the cost.

Cautiously he left his covert and stole round to the back of the house, thus shielding himself from all chance of discovery by anyone coming from the ranche.

Behind the house, fastened to a tree, Manuel found two horses; he recognised them at once as being from the stable of Torres, and guessed rightly that they were the two that had conveyed the fugitives.

Approaching the hut with the caution of the panther stealing upon its prey, Manuel discovered a little opening in the timbers by which he commanded a full view of the interior apartment. The room contained Ruy Lara and Rita.

When Ruy Lara entered the room, with a scream of joy Rita had flung herself into his arms.

"You are come at last!" she cried.

"Yes, dear one," he replied, soothingly. "Did you fancy that I was never coming?"

"I have not seen you for so long," said the girl, sorrowfully.

"Why, it is but a few hours since I had you in my arms," he answered.

"The time has seemed very long to me," she said, mournfully.

"Cheer up, Rita," he said, imprinting warm kisses on her fresh, red lips. "Now I am by your side, never again to part from you."

"That makes me feel so happy," said the girl, looking up into his face, trustingly. "When you are by my side I feel in paradise; when I am alone I have no desire to live. We shall be happy now, shall we not?" she asked, reclining trustfully on his breast.

"Happy!" he exclaimed. "Yes, as happy as the day is long." Then his warm kisses again pressed the dewy lips—kisses that were given back with interest. For the moment they were happy—happy in the happiest of all dreams—love.

The sudden opening of the door rudely disturbed the lovers. Ruy Lara was, by a powerful arm, stricken to the floor, even as he had been stricken by the American, though this time the blow was not quite so heavy, or so skilfully struck. He still retained his senses only to see over him the frowning face of Manuel, the herdsman, and to feel his knife's point in his throat.

CHAPTER IX.

A RIDE FOR LIFE.

FULLY did Lara comprehend the peril of his position. He could feel the sharp point of the keen-edged knife pricking the skin of his throat.

"Utter one sound of alarm, Rita, and with my knife I'll let out the blood of this hound and give his soul to the Devil, it's master!" cried the Pathfinder; and Ruy, as he looked into the fierce eyes that glared so threateningly into his own, felt that the Indian was indeed in savage earnest. The fierce light gleamed in his eyes like that of a cougar when it is about to spring upon its prey.

"Oh, my brother, spare him!" cried the peon girl, stretching out her hands imploringly.

"Listen to me, sister," he answered. "I am about to take you from this wolf. If you refuse to go, I'll kill him on the spot, as I would kill any beast of prey."

"No, no," she cried; "spare him. I will go with you."

"I will spare him on one condition: that you go with me quietly, and without any attempt to return to him; but, first to secure this dog, so that he cannot give the alarm after our departure. Bring the blanket from the bed."

Rita obeyed his order, trembling with excitement and fear.

"Take my knife and cut it into narrow strips, three or four inches wide," the Pathfinder continued, giving her the knife, at the same time drawing a revolver, which he placed in close proximity to the temples of the Mexican.

Ruy made no attempt at resistance; though young and powerful of muscle, he felt that he was no match for the desperate brother, who needed but slight provocation to redden his knife with the betrayer's blood.

Then taking the strips which the peon girl had cut, the Indian bound first the hands and then the feet of the Mexican, rendering him as helpless and as powerless as an infant; and, as a final precaution, the peon rolled up a piece of the blanket in the form f a ball, and with a strip of the same fastened the ball securely in Ruy's mouth, thus gagging him most effectually. Lara, after the Indian had finished his task, could neither move nor speak.

The Pathfinder then cast a hasty glance through the door. No one was in sight.

"Come," he said to his sister sternly; "I will take you far from this den of infamy, and from this man who would destroy you."

With one farewell glance at the one whom she so idolised, and without a word, Rita followed her brother to the horses. The chance of escaping unseen was desperate; they must pass within full view of the ranche. The Pathfinder felt that their only hope lay in the speed of their steeds.

By the side of the beasts Manuel spoke again.

"Rita," he said, "I know that you are blind to your own good. I know that this Mexican snake has fascinated you to your ruin. I have sworn by the bones of our mother that I will save you from him. If you attempt to escape from me I'll kill you with my own hand." And Rita fully realised that her brother, usually so mild and gentle, was now terribly in earnest, and would surely keep his word.

Once mounted, they proceeded slowly past the house. Beyond it lay the open space over which he must cross to gain the prairies, full in view from the ranche.

"Be ready, sister. for a sharp gallop," he said, as

they entered upon the open space. No one was in sight. The heart of the Pathfinder beat high with hope; he had gained the edge of the prairie, when, through the door of the stockade came a noisy group —a half-dozen or so of the brigands. The instant their eyes fell upon the peons they comprehended that something was wrong; they knew that their young chief had a girl in the little log-house, yet here she was on the prairie with a stranger, apparently flying.

With a wild yell some of the brigands rushed to the stable for horses; other fled to the log-house to discover what had become of Lara, to find him bound and gagged. They released him at once.

Wild with rage, Ruy sprang to his feet.

"Horses!" he cried. "Pursue them at once!" then dashed from the house.

'Twas the custom of the brigands to keep a dozen horses or so saddled, at all times, ready for any emergencies; so that Ruy, rushing from the house, found the horses ready on the prairie.

Snatching a carbine from one of the men, Ruy vaulted into the saddle, and, at the head of ten of the brigands armed to the teeth, rode after the fast-flying fugitives.

So quick had been all these movements—so little time had they taken, that the peons had hardly ten minutes' start; and, on the broad, open prairie, here with scarcely a hillock to obstruct the view, they could easily be seen at a distance of five miles, instead of the two which separated them from their pursuers.

On went the chase—each party urging their horses to the utmost.

Five—ten miles have the horses of the pursued and the pursuers passed over. Then, turning in the saddle, the Pathfinder measured the distance between

himself and his pursuers. The brigands were gaining ground! and his ear catching the heavy breathing
of his horse, convinced him that the pace was telling
hard upon the animal.

"A few miles more and they will overtake us,
murmured the Pathfinder, between his teeth.
"Caramba!" and he hissed out the oath from his
firm-clenched teeth, "if I die, other blood beside mine
will redden the prairie. My poor beast is nearly done
for; I've a mind to pull up and make a fight for it;
there's not more than a dozen, and my rifle and
revolver are good for six lives to say nothing of my
knife."

And what were Rita's thoughts? Alas, poor girl,
her heart was so full of anguish that thought had
almost ceased. She knew full well that, in the event
of a conflict, she must lose either a lover or a brother,
or both must perish. The beautiful but hapless girl
wished that she was in her grave.

"Caramba!" cried the bandit chief in glee, as he
saw that he was gaining upon the fugitives; "another
half-hour and we shall overtake them."

"Their horses are tiring," cried Tio, who rode next
to Ruy, foremost in the chase.

"Yes; their horses are winded, while ours, as yet,
are fresh," responded Ruy.

"Capitano, will not this peon be likely to show
fight?" asked one of the brigands, a huge red-headed
fellow, who answered to the name of Legro.

"Well, are we not ten to one?" demanded Ruy.
"If the dog shows his teeth, we'll pull them out for
him."

At which piece of pleasantry the brigands in hear-
ing laughed loud and long.

"Ah, comrade!" cried Tio, quietly to himself, "the
process of extracting teeth of yonder dog may be

more difficult than you imagine, and may cost more
lives than one. By the beard of my grandfather, if
there is to be a fight he'll not be apt to spare me,
that's certain ; so for the present, my place is in the
rear." And having come to this conclusion, Tio,
without attracting attention, quickly tightened the
rein on his horse and let the others pass him. He
soon was the rearmost rider. Intent upon the chase,
none of the brigands noticed this little manœuvre.
Safely located in the rear, Tio chuckled to himself.

"Now, then," he cried, jocosely addressing his
speech to the animal on whose back he sat, " let the
sport begin as soon as possible ; you and I are out of
danger. But may the good Mother of God protect
that brave soul !" he ejaculated, with real fervour.

Still hotly on, riding for life, pressed the pursued,
and still hotly on their track followed the brigands.

A stumble, and the horse of the peon went down
upon his knees. A yell of joy burst from the hoarse
throats of the pursuers. Quickly, however, the
practised hand of the Indian pulled the horse to his
feet, and still onward over the prairie went the race
for life.

" This cannot last much longer !" cried the peon,
as he noted how rapidly his enemies were gaining
upon him, and what signs of distress and exhaustion
his horse was showing.

Eagerly the hunted man surveyed the broad
prairie. Mile upon mile it stretched on, one vast,
unbroken plain. It never before looked so boundless
and forbidding !"

What would not the Pathfinder have given then for
one little clump of timber—a single wooded knoll—
in which he might seek shelter—which he might turn
into a fortress, and from its cover defy its foes !

He felt that he was doomed, and only for the iron

will that clenched his firm-set teeth, he would have groaned aloud in agony. Then, when he looked upon his sister, the knowledge that his death would give her again into the hands of the man he hated, Ruy Lara, the Mexican, was maddening.

Convulsively, the Pathfinder loosened the knife in his belt; the dread thought was in his heart; he would kill her rather than she should fall the prey of the man who had charmed her as the serpent charms the bird.

"Yes," thought the desperate brother, while still he rode furiously onward, "I will stab her with my own hand, if the worst comes, for there is no other way to save her. Surely, our parents will look down from heaven and bless the deed! It is not murder; it is but saving the lamb from the wolf."

CHAPTER X.
THE COUGAR SHOWS HIS TEETH.

"PREPARE your weapons, men!" shouted Ruy.

It was evident to the brigand that a few minutes more would give the fugitives into his hands.

Eagerly the brigands unslung their carbines. Human bloodhounds, this chase, which must end in death, was to them but pastime.

Tio, safe in the rear, watched the proceeding with interest.

"By Old Nick himself, the patron saint of these fellows, but this will be as rare fun as a bull-fight," he cried.

Again the brave Pathfinder's horse stumbled and went down upon his knees.

"By heaven!" cried Ruy, "he's thrown!"

And it was apparently so, for when the horse rose to his feet his master had disappeared from his back, and the pursuers could just discern a dark mass, evidently the form of the Pathfinder, extended upon the prairie.

A yell of joy burst from the throats of the brigands at the sight.

"Bah!" cried Tio, disgusted, "there is to be no fight, then, after all—no fight! I wanted to see half-a-dozen of these fellows laid out on the prairie. Well, there's one consolation, there'll be more for the soldiers to kill."

Rita had dismounted, apparently to help her brother, and yet Ruy noticed, as he rode towards them, that she remained standing by her horse, not twenty paces from the prostrate man.

The brigand suspected some ruse. The thought struck him how improbable it was that the herdsman—notoriously one of the best riders for miles around, and used from boyhood to taming wild steeds of the prairie—should be thrown from a tired horse, and knocked senseless, too, by contact with the prairie's soft surface. Instinctively Ruy slackened the speed of his horse; the brigands, with a sort of vague apprehension or danger, followed his example.

The ruffians were now within rifle-range of the Pathfinder, and were approaching at a gentle gallop. Tio, still in the rear, and scenting danger from afar, had slackened the pace of his horse into a walk.

Suddenly, then, from under the belly of the peon's horse—which was standing broadside to the brigands—came a little puff of white smoke; the sharp report of a rifle followed, and the brigand who rode just behind Ruy reeled in his saddle, clutched vacantly at the air, and tumbled from his horse, shot through the breast. Ruy saw that the shot had been aimed at him.

"Bravo!" cried Tio, safe in the rear; "the l

finder begins to show his teeth. Now draw them,
senor brigands, and may the devil get you all !''

Maddened with rage, Ruy rose in his stirrups.
"Forward !" he cried. " Shoot down the man, but
spare the girl !"

The brigands rushed onward, impatient to avenge
their comrade's death.

" Reserve your fire till within pistol range !" cried
Ruy. " He is defenceless ; don't let him escape !
Make this his last trail !"

As the brigands galloped rapidly towards him—
reserving their fire in obedience to the orders of their
leader—the moment they got within revolver-range
the intrepid and self-possessed peon opened fire.
Crack ! crack ! crack ! Three little puffs of white
smoke, the three sharp reports, and three brigands
tumbled from their saddles, one shot dead— pierced
through the temple ; the other two badly wounded.

Instinctively, and without waiting for orders, the
riders pulled up their horses and discharged a scatter-
ing fire upon their desperate game. But, so confused
was their aim, that not a single shot struck the peon
or his horse, behind whose body he was now shel-
tered.

The brigands had halted on receiving the deadly
fire, and two or three showed a disposition to retreat. Almost mad with rage, and wild at the
thought of losing four of his followers, Ruy urged
them on.

" Cowards !" he cried, " will you retreat from one
man ? On and crush him !"

But his men hesitated ; they had guessed, from
the rapidity of the fire. that the Pathfinder was
armed with a revolver, that wonderful North American weapon of which they had heard so much and
knew so little

At this moment the hunted peon again opened fire. Twice he discharged the revolver, thus emptying the chambers of the weapon. Each shot was aimed at Ruy Lara, for, could he disable that ruffian, the others would retreat. The second shot toppled Lara from the saddle. The Pathfinder gave vent to a fierce shout of joy, which was answered by a cry of dismay from the attacking party—the members of which speedily retreated out of range, bearing their stricken leader with them. Fortune, however, favoured the brigand chief, for the ball merely passed through the fleshy part of the shoulder, making but a slight wound.

"Are you hurt?" inquired red-bearded Legro, as he paused with the wounded leader at a safe distance from the deadly fire of the peon.

"Not seriously; the ball has only cut through my shoulder. My horse, starting at the moment, caused me to lose my seat," answered Ruy, as he sprung into the saddle again.

"*Caramba!*" cried the peon, in despair; "Satan himself aids this man. Four times have I missed him."

Rita, who had been watching the combat with straining eyes, now fearing for her brother, now for her lover, opposed to each other in this deadly combat, when she saw the brigand leader fall—dead, she imagined—killed by the ball from her brother's pistol—could not endure the fatal sight; her senses failed, and, with a faint shriek, she fell apparently lifeless upon the ground.

The moment the brigands retreated, the Pathfinder proceeded to reload his weapons. His rifle loaded, he felt in his pouch for the bullets of the revolver, when, to his dismay, he discovered that he had nothing but rifle bullets, too large to fit the other weapon.

D 2

"By the Virgin!" he cried, in dismay, "my revolver is useless. I have but my rifle—one shot— one life, and they are yet seven to one. Should they make another attack I am lost. I'll load the barrels with powder, though ; the dog may frighten with his bark if he cannot bite. In an hour the sun will be down ; night will come ; if I can but baffle them till then, amid the shadows of darkness I can escape."

Loud and hot was the discussion among the Mexicans. They already had lost four men out of eleven, which left but seven in the field, and one of these—Ruy, their leader—was already wounded.

"If you had closed in upon him when I ordered, he would now be in our power or lifeless," cried Ruy, bitterly.

"Pardon, capitano!" cried Legro, who was a sort of a leader among the brigands, though bearing no rank. "The fiend is armed with revolvers ; besides we'd emptied our pieces, and before we could have cut him down with our sabres, he could easily have shot us down, one by one. He shoots with wonderful skill, that I'll swear."

"Bah!" cried Ruy, in anger; "he had fired five shots ; that is the number of chambers a revolver has ; the chances are a hundred to one that he was helpless when we retreated."

"Perhaps," growled Legro, sullenly ; but, then, he may have two or three more revolvers, and what man wants to run into certain death ? I fear no living man, but I don't want to be shot down like a dog in cold blood, without a chance for my life."

"Yes, yes, that's true; that's so !" came from the lips of three or four of the brigands, who felt but little relish to again encounter the Pathfinder with his death-dealing weapons at close quarters.

"It is clearly impossible to gain anything by making a direct attack," said Ruy, musingly.

"Oh, clearly!" cried Legro, and the rest of the band echoed his words.

"In a short time night will come," said Ruy.

"Yes, and then good-bye to all hopes of killing this viper," responded Legro. "In the darkness he can easily escape. He knows the prairie like a bee, and will disappear like a snake."

"Could we not place sentinels around and so hem him in?" asked another of the band.

"No!" cried Ruy. "At whatever part of the line he attempted to break through, he would find but one man to oppose him. One shot then would open the way for the peon's flight. I have a plan, though, that may succeed."

And eagerly the brigands gathered around to listen.

CHAPTER XI.
THE WOLF AT BAY.

"My plan is simple," said the leader. "Before we failed because we all attacked together in one body and from one point. Now, my idea is to surround and attack him from *all* points. His attention being thus diverted, for he cannot watch all of us at once, someone of our number may be able to disable him, or, at all events, disable the horses. That would place him without means of escape.

"Now," continued Ruy, "there are seven of us here. We will form a circle around him, keeping out of range of his fire. Then, when the circle is complete, we will all dash in upon him simultaneously. I will give the signal for the advance by discharging my pistol. Remember, disable the horses if you can, not the man; and do not expose yourselves recklessly to the fire. We cannot afford to lose more men."

Which caution was entirely unnecessary, for none of the cut-throats had any desire to expose their precious lives within range of the peon's deadly fire.

"Now, then, prepare for the attack!" cried Ruy. "Tio, you remain here; this will be your station. The rest follow me. Remember, men, the signal for the advance is a shot from my pistol."

And Tio was left, much to his own satisfaction, just where he proposed to remain—out of rifle-reach.

Ruy, with the brigands, galloped off to form the circle—which would soon be a circle of fire, eager to consume its prey—around the death-doomed man.

Some five hundred yards or so, Legro dropped out of the ranks and took his station there; the rest of the band rode on. Another five hundred yards another brigand stopped, and so they went on, until, at last, Ruy alone was left to gallop onward. Then he, too, stopped, wheeled his horse around to face the prey, and the peon was completely encircled by the prairie bandits.

This manœuvre had not been unobserved by the Pathfinder; he understood its meaning only too well.

"Ah, the cowards!" he cried. "They intend to dash in upon me as the Indians surround and dash in upon the wild buffaloes. I fear my race is run. I am almost powerless for defence, too; one load in my rifle is but one life. If I had my revolver charged, I'd make some of them rue the attempt to ride me down like a wild beast. But let them come!" cried the brave brother, defiantly, as he drew back the hammer of his rifle and levelled it across the back of the horse, direct at Ruy. "*He* will never touch Rita's hand again."

The brigand captain looked around the cordon of

men; motionless they sat in the saddle, carbine in hand, waiting for the signal.

Sharp and shrill rung out on the air the report of Lara's pistol.

Seven horses felt the spur-stroke of seven pair of heels, and the brigands rode into the attack.

Narrow grew the circle as they closed in upon the prey.

The Pathfinder reserved his fire till Lara was fairly within range; then the sharp report of his rifle broke upon the air. Full at Ruy Lara's heart had the ball been aimed, but the brigand captain was fated not there to die. The chief had caught the glint of the fast-dying sun on the shining rifle-tube—had guessed the moment of the discharge, and, causing his horse to rear, the beast had received the ball full in his chest, and, with a convulsive groan, had fallen upon his knees, then rolled over on his side, mortally wounded. Ruy nimbly disengaged his feet from the stirrups, and, as the beast fell, leaped from his back to the ground. Losing his balance, however, he fell prostrate.

A wild whoop rung from the lips of the peon as he witnessed the fall and supposed death of his enemy. Quickly levelling the revolver and wheeling upon the foe advancing in his rear, he fired. The blank charge was as fully effectual in one sense as if it had contained a ball, for the brigands advancing in that direction turned their horses about and retreated far more rapidly than they had advanced.

Wheeling quickly, the Pathfinder fired first at the brigands approaching on the right, then at those on the left. Panic-stricken at their leader's fall, they fired their pieces at random at the single foe; then, following the example of the others, retreated fast across the prairie.

Ruy, by this time, had gained his feet.

A cry of rage broke from Manuel's lips.

"Is this man a fiend," he cried, "that I cannot kill him?"

And what would not the peon have given to have had his loaded rifle in his hand again—to have had one more chance at the life of his foe!

Ruy snatched up his carbine from the ground, where it had been thrown by the shock of his fall. On foot then, carbine in hand, reckless of the consequence, he dashed in upon the peon, as though single-handed he would crush him; but there was method in the madness of the leader. The moment he arrived within range he leveled his carbine and fired; the shot struck the Pathfinder's horse just behind the shoulder; the wound was mortal, and the horse sunk upon the prairie, striken unto death.

Manuel discharged two barrels of the really harmless revolver at the brigand, and he, thinking that he heard the whistling of the balls about his head, and conscious that he had deprived the peon of the means of flight, retreated across the prairie to where the brigands, all assembled together and well out of reach of the peon's fire, were watching the mad movements of their leader. But when they saw the horse of the peon fall—saw Ruy retreat unharmed, they sent forth a shout of triumph; they admired fool-hardiness in others, though they had but little inclination to indulge in it themselves.

Thanks to the blank cartridges in the Indian's revolver, Ruy Lara rejoined his band unharmed.

"Catch me a horse, some of you," he said.

A brigand dashed off in chase of one of the riderless horses. The horses had not strayed far, and the fellow speedily returned with one.

Ruy, again in the saddle, prepared to assail the single foe who still so bravely held his own.

"That was a daring attempt, capitano!" cried Legro, in admiration.

"If you had but closed in upon him, the affair would have been ended," replied Ruy; "but, as it is, I have cut off his retreat; one horse remains for the two; either he must abandon the girl or sacrifice his own life."

"Why, capitano, the bullets of this red devil seem to have no effect upon you. Twice he has failed to kill you," said Legro.

"I was not born to die by the hand of a peon!" exclaimed Ruy, scornfully.

"Recharge your pieces, you that have fired. We'll dash in upon him again. If we cannot kill him we can disable the other horse, and then he is wholly in our power."

The brigands who had fired proceeded to reload.

The carbines charged, again they gather round their leader to receive his last instructions.

The Pathfinder, who had reloaded his weapons, still using but powder alone for his revolver, for want of bullets, had waited patiently for some new movement on the part of his relentless foes. By the death of his horse he was uncovered on that side to the fire of the attacking party.

A sigh escaping from his sister's lips aroused him. Rita was recovering from her swoon. The brother hastened to her side; the brigands were still quiet, apparently holding a council.

"Is he dead?" were the first words that came from the lips of the peon girl.

"No; he is unharmed; the Evil One protects him," answered the brother.

"And you have not been wounded?" she asked.

"No; but the struggle will soon be over. The next attack will probably cost me my life; then you will be free to go with this man for whom you are willing to peril your soul."

"Oh, my brother!" cried the girl, rising to her feet, "would that I had been dead and in my quiet grave ere I had brought you into this peril."

"Would you rather die with me than lead a life of shame?" questioned Manuel, sternly, drawing, at the same moment, the keen-edged knife from his belt.

"No no, brother!" cried Rita, sinking upon her knees with uplifted hand; "I am not prepared to die; do not kill me, spare me. Let me not make you a murderer!"

"Spare you!" exclaimed the Pathfinder; "spare you, so that when I am cold in death you will rush to the arms of this fiend? Spare you, so that you may bring disgrace to the blood of your dead mother? No!"

Manuel seized her by the hand, and the shining blade of the long knife glittered in her eyes.

"Ask Heaven to forgive you your sins!" he cried, as he raised the knife to give the death-blow.

CHAPTER XII.
THE MASTERS OF THE PRAIRIE.

"Spare me! spare me, brother!" implored the kneeling girl, and then her eyes wandered wildly across the prairie towards the brigands, as though she expected that help would come from them to save her from her brother's steel.

"See!" she cried suddenly. "They are retreating! See, Manuel, brother, they are flying!"

Astonished at this sudden manœuvre, the Pathfinder turned his gaze upon his foes.

The girl had spoken the truth; the brigands were in full retreat. Spurring their horses, like men mad, they were flying at their topmost speed across the prairie.

"Strange!" I cannot understand the meaning of this, cried the peon, as he watched the rapid and unceremonious flight of his foes. "What can have caused it?" Then the peon swept his eye around the horizon to see if he could discover the reason for this unaccountable proceeding on the part of the brigands.

The Pathfinder's searching glance soon discovered a body of horsemen advancing from the west.

"Are the very powers of evil against me?" he cried.

"What is it?" exclaimed Rita, gazing in astonishment into her brother's face.

"See there!" he cried, pointing to the body of horsemen advancing from the west.

"I see a body of horsemen advancing rapidly."

"Yes, they ride with the speed of the wind," gloomily replied the peon.

"Dear brother, you are saved then!"

"No, I am lost!" returned Manuel.

"Lost!" cried Rita in astonishment.

"Yes; we are both lost!" despairingly cried the peon. "Look again! Can you not guess who they are?"

"They are not Mexicans, for they do not wear sombreros," said the girl, still shading her eyes with her hands and gazing intently at the fast-approaching strangers. "They are not North Americans, for I cannot see the gleam of their sabres."

"Would to heaven that they were the soldiers of the Republic; then we should be saved. Now we are lost!" returned the dejected man.

The dark mass had now approached so near that, to the eyes of the girl, it began to separate into single horsemen. "They are Indians!" she cried suddenly.

"Yes, Comanches," returned her brother. " 'Tis a foray against the frontier. It was their appearance that caused the speedy retreat of the Mexicans."

"What can we do?" questioned Rita.

"Nothing. In a few minutes we shall be prisoners in their hands. Resistance is useless, and would only exasperate them."

"What will be our fate?" asked Rita anxiously.

"You will become the wife of some chief, and they will make a slave of me."

"Oh, such a fate will be terrible!" cried Rita in anguish.

"It is our destiny; we are doomed," cried Manuel. "But in their hands as prisoners, there is still a chance for escape. The Indians evidently are about to attack some frontier town, perhaps Tacos; if so, the soldiers there—of whom they can have no knowledge—will give them a warm reception, and we stand a faint chance of release; therefore do not breathe a word of the presence of the North Americans in the village."

"I will not," replied Rita. "I would do anything —dare anything to escape from this dreadful fate."

On came the red warriors, the masters of the prairie, sweeping down upon the two peons as the eagle sweeps down upon its prey.

On they came at the best speed of their hardy little ponies, gaily adorned with the bright war-paint, and the many-coloured feathers that formed their headdresses and fluttered from their long lances waving proudly in the wind.

It was quite a large war-party, numbering, perhaps, fifty warriors, led, too, by chiefs of note.

The party were on the yearly foray against the Mexican frontier settlements. Their course was to be marked with blood, and the smoke and flame of the burning ruins that they left in their track.

It was apparent that the party had not struck a blow yet, for no trophies of victory adorned their persons. They had probably crossed the Rio Grande below El Paso and struck inland to avoid observation.

Upon approaching within rifle-shot of the peons, the warriors separated, and, branching out to the right and left, enclosed the two in a circle, and then halted.

The Pathfinder discharged his rifle in the air. His revolver he had previously cast down in the grass, so that it should not fall into their hands ; then he drew the knife from his belt and threw it far from him on the prairie, and held out his hands signifying that he was unarmed.

Two of the Indians, apparently the chiefs of the party, advanced.

As a rule, the wild master of the prairie despises his " civilised " brother, the Mexican, and not without reason. But the two chiefs, having noted the bodies of the slain brigands, had quickly arrived at a correct solution of the situation.

The two chiefs who now approached were strikingly alike in person, though one was old and the other young—evidently father and son.

" Did my red brother kill these men ? " asked the elder chief, speaking excellent Spanish.

" Yes," replied the peon.

" Alone ?"

" Yes."

" Wah !" ejaculated the young chief. " My brother is a great brave."

" Does my brother live in the lodges of the Mexicans ?" asked the old chief.

" Yes," the peon answered.

" Yet they are dogs, and try to kill him !"

"A man may have foes even among the people in whose lodges he dwells," said the herdsman.

"My brother speaks straight; his skin is red—his heart is not white. Why will he live in the lodges of the pale-faces?"

"He was born there," responded Manuel.

"Let him be born again, and this time a Comanche," said the old chief, tersely.

"It is good," said the other chief, "the Iron-pan is a great chief; he will be a brother to the red warrior who has dwelt in the lodges of the pale-faces."

"And the Grey Bear will be his father," said the old chief; and then his eyes falling upon the girl, he asked, "Squaw?"

"No; sister," replied Manuel.

"Wah! she is as fair as a prairie-flower," said the old chief.

Rita at heart trembled at the compliment, though outwardly she preserved her calmness.

"Does my brother know of white lodges by the big river there?" and the old chief pointed southwest in the direction of Tacos.

"Yes; Tacos," said Manuel.

"Ugh! good!" said the Grey Bear. "My brother will lead my warriors there?"

"Yes," Manuel promptly replied.

"How long?" questioned the chief.

"We shall reach there before light in the morning," Manuel answered.

"It is good!" answered the chief. "Let my red brother take his rifle again. The Comanchos are his brothers; he is a great warrior. The Grey Bear will fight for the Long-rifle," the Indian had already named the new recruit to the Comanche ranks.

So, a horse was brought and the Pathfinder

mounted and set out with the old chief in advance of the war-party. Rita was placed in the centre of the warriors. And so they took up their line of march for Tacos.

CHAPTER XIII.
THE ATTACK ON TACOS.

WE will return now to Lieutenant Wenie. When he received Juanita's note on his return from his expedition down the river, his consternation was great. Wenie saw plainly that his love for Juanita was suspected by her father, and that he had taken the girl away to prevent her communicating with him. What was to be done?

Vainly he pondered over the affair. The Mexicans had four or five hours' start; should he follow in pursuit? and then what excuse had he should he overtake them? True. he loved Juanita, and she loved him. but he could not very well take her by force from the arms and protection of her own father.

The lieutenant was puzzled; he resolved to seek the advice of Major Curtin. Repairing to the major's quarters, he found him there as usual.

Briefly to the major the young officer explained matters—related how he had met the senorita on the prairie, and how she had agreed to become his wife; and, lastly, he told of the flight of Torres and his daughter, and showed the major the note he had received.

The old soldier read the little note carefully.

"It is evident," he said, thoughtfully, " that the girl loves you."

"I'd stake my life upon her truth!" cried Wenie, warmly.

"Well, I believe you could do so with safety,"

replied the major. "It is plain that the girl takes after her mother, who was a good woman, and not after her father, who is a black-hearted scoundrel. I am fully satisfied, Wenie, that that man knows something of the fate of my lost boy, and one of these days—not far distant either—I may have him in so tight a place that he will gladly tell all he knows."

"But, major, what do you advise me to do?" asked Wenie.

"At present—nothing," was the major's curt reply.

"Nothing!" cried Wenie in astonishment.

"Nothing," repeated the major. "What else can you do? You can't follow on this man's track with a body of United States soldiers, and say to him: 'I love your daughter; give her to me or I'll take her.' There's nothing in the Army Regulations that provides for any *such* action as that."

"True, true!" replied Wenie; "you are right, major. But if they take her to Santa Fe, there they may force her to marry this Ruy Lara that I have told you of," said Wenie.

"Well, in the first place," replied the major, thoughtfully, "I do not think that there is any danger that the girl will be taken to Santa Fe; and then, the next thing is to force the girl to consent to the marriage, and, from your description of the lady, I fancy that it will be no easy matter. They are not likely to use actual violence in the affair, though I have no doubt that both of these men are capable of it. Take my word for it, she will not be taken very far from here, and they will have to keep a close watch upon her to keep her from communicating with you."

"Then you think that she will contrive in some y to let me know where she is?" said Wenie.

"Precisely so," remarked the major. "But, lieu-tenant, you need not remain entirely quiet and do nothing. You can bribe some Mexican in the village here to visit Torres' hacienda on some pretext, and in a careless way question the servants and the in-mates of the house in regard to the whereabouts of Torres and his daughter. In that way you might be able to pick up some information of value to you."

" Your suggestion is good, major. I will act upon it the first thing in the morning," said Wenie, rising to depart.

" By the way, lieutenant," said the major, " I have discovered where the hiding-place of these brigands is located."

" Indeed!" cried Wenie, in astonishment.

" Yes ; a secluded ranche on the bank of the Rio Pecos. I have a rude map of the road thither, and of the defences of the place. It's quite a strong place, defended by a stockade wall, impregnable except against artillery or a sudden and unlooked-for attack."

"When do you propose to move against them?" asked Wenie.

"As soon as I receive further information. My spy is even now in the brigands' stronghold."

" Is it possible? " exclaimed Wenie. " He must be a daring fellow. But good-night, major."

" Good-night, lieutenant," returned the older officer, and Wenie repaired to his own quarters.

The lieutenant's slumbers that night were far from pleasant ; his rest was broken by confused dreams ; and when the morning came and he awoke, he felt but little refreshed by his night's rest.

The morning duties over, Wenie sought among the Mexicans of the village for a messenger to visit the hacienda of Torres, there to gain tidings, if possi-ble. of Torres or his daughter.

The messenger was soon found, who, for a golden ounce—to him a fortune—undertook to perform the task.

After receiving his instructions from the lieutenant, the Mexican departed on his mission.

Long seemed the hours to the lieutenant, until the Mexican returned, which event occurred about noon.

The messenger had learned comparatively nothing —that is, nothing that could give the anxious lover a clue to the destination of his beloved Juanita.

The Mexican told the lieutenant of the sudden departure of Torres and his daughter, and an escort, for Santa Fe; the halt at the ruined ranche and the appearance of Ruy Lara and his armed followers; then, how the escort from the hacienda was sent back, and how Torres and his daughter had proceeded on their way with Ruy and his men.

Wenie paid the Mexican his promised fee—much to that worthy's delight, which he showed by instantly going and getting gloriously drunk; and the lieutenant went to the major's quarters to tell him what he had learned.

Curtin listened attentively. When Wenie had finished, for a moment he remained silent; then he abruptly said:

"Lieutenant, it is as I suspected. I did not want to tell you of my suspicions last night, because I had really no good reasons for them, and I thought you felt bad enough without my saying anything to make you feel worse."

"What do you suspect?" asked Wenie, in alarm.

"Well, lieutenant, I hardly suspect now; I am sure of it. The story of the appearance of this Lara at the ruined ranche with a body of armed men, opens my eyes at once. This Lara, lieutenant, is one of the principal leaders of the Brigands of the Prairie;

Torres, as I suspected, is secretly in league with the brigands. The armed men that Ruy Lara headed were the brigands themselves."

"Then you think—" and Wenic hesitated to utter the fearful words.

"I think," said the major, slowly, "that the girl Juanita is now at the stronghold of the brigands on the Rio Pecos."

"Then we have an excuse to rescue her," cried the lieutenant, a gleam of joy lighting up his features; "we can attack these villains, destroy them, and free her; that is strictly in the line of our duty."

"You are right!" exclaimed the major, "and we will perform that duty. I should have preferred to wait until I heard again from my spy; but, as it is, the case will hardly bear delay; therefore, we will set out at once. The brigands' stronghold is, I should judge, a score of leagues from here; but, by crowding the horses, we can reach it by sunrise. The attack must be a surprise, or else within their stockade they might be able to hold us at bay. I will give the orders instantly for the movement."

But, as the major rose from his chair, a Mexican, breathless with haste, rushed into the room.

"What the deuce do you want?" cried Curtin, annoyed at the unceremonious entrance.

"Oh, senor major!" cried the Mexican, and then paused for breath.

"Well, what is it?"

"The Indians! the Comanches!"

"What?" And the major started in astonishment.

"Oh, senor, they are on their way to attack us— a large war-party—a hundred warriors!" cried the Mexican.

And then, when the messenger had recovered his breath, he told how, hunting after stray cattle on the upper Rio Grande, concealed in the shrubbery by the river's bank, he had seen the Indians cross the river, and strike inland.   Tacos, being the nearest town, was, of course, the objective point of the expedition; and the Mexican hastened at once to give the alarm.

"This puts a stop to our expedition, lieutenant," said the major, "for we must attend to these red demons first. We'll give them such a reception that the story of it shall strike terror throughout their tribe. It is very evident that they do not know of our presence here. They will not attack us till about midnight or early morning—that is their favourite hour. To-night, Wenie, we'll attend to these redskins, to-morrow to the yellow-birds."

So the major and lieutenant went forth to prepare for the expected attack.

Each house received its complement of soldiers; those at the north end of the town, the point supposed to be the first likely to feel the Indian attack, had a double number. Forty men were ambushed in the houses—the remaining twenty were posted in the corral back of the mission, ready to mount and dash upon the savages upon their retreat from the cross-fire of the houses.

When the shades of night descended upon the village, few would have supposed, so calm and quiet was the street, that each dwelling was a fortress bristling with weapons and teeming with armed men.

The hours passed rapidly on; midnight came; the major and the lieutenant made a final inspection of their men, urging increased caution. Not a gun was to be fired until a shot from the major's revolver gave the signal for the attack.

The major himself took post upon the flat roof of

the mission-house, lying at full length behind the low railing. Concealed from sight, he commanded a full view of the single street upon which Tacos was built.

The hours passed slowly away; the first grey streaks of the coming morn began to line the eastern clouds, when, to the watching ears of the major, came the tramp of many hoofs. A few minutes more, and the street below was filled with dark forms.

The Comanches had come.

The morning light was in the eastern sky when the Indians entered Tacos. No sound of alarm had been given, the town was apparently buried in slumber.

The Comanches gained the little square before the mission-house, the centre of the town; then, rising in his rude stirrups, the Grey Bear gave the loud war-whoop, the signal for slaughter. Hardly had the sound of the loud war-cry of the red chief broke on the still morning air, when it was answered by the shrill crack of a revolver. Up into the air convulsively went the arms of the Grey Bear; he reeled from the saddle, and fell headlong to the earth, a lifeless mass.

Hardly had the crack of the revolver answered the yell of the Indian, when a sheet of flame burst from each side of the little street, and the carbine balls came thick and deadly among the red warriors. Panic-stricken, they turned to fly, hardly returning the fire of the soldiers. But the major, heading the squad of mounted men, dashed upon them; the soldiers poured from the houses; and the Comanches, disdaining to ask for quarter, were cut down like sheep in the slaughter-pen, and of the band that rode so boldly to the attack on Tacos, hardly ten of them ever crossed the Rio Grande to bear back to their tribe the story of their defeat by the blue-coated chiefs in the street of the little Mexican village.

The loss of the soldiers was but slight—a single man killed and ten or so slightly wounded. Few of the Indians being armed with fire arms, accounted for the slight loss on the part of the troops.

But the Pathfinder and his sister—where were they? They were not among the ten who fled, or the party that lay wounded or dead.

CHAPTER XIV.
A DESPERATE GAME.

THE pistol-shot of the major warned the Pathfinder that in some way the soldiers had learned of the approach of the savages, and were prepared to receive them. As they had ridden into the town, Manuel had endeavoured to elude the vigilance of the Indians, by whom he was surrounded, and give some alarm to arouse the citizens and soldiers; but the savages kept a wary eye upon him, and he felt that the attempt would cost him his life, and not be of much service to his friends. He felt sure that the soldiers, once aroused, could easily beat off the Indians. So he wisely rode quietly into the place. The single shot revealed to him the trap that the Comanches had so unwittingly stumbled into.

To think was to act, with Manuel. Instantly he tumbled out of the saddle to the ground, just in time to escape the bullets hurled so thickly into the ranks of the Indians. The moment he struck the ground he ran to the shelter of the nearest house, and there remained till the brief fight had ended. He knew that all efforts of his in behalf of his sister would be fruitless, and he trusted to Heaven to protect her, and a good Providence answered the expectation.

The escape of Rita was almost miraculous. In the centre of the savages, their bodies were the ramparts that shielded her from the deadly fire that mowed them down as the grain falls before the sickle; and then the fiery Indian pony that she rode, scared by the fire arms, carried her rapidly up the street, far from the scene of slaughter. She could not control the beast, so, with a prayer upon her lips, she leaped boldly from his back. The soft earth received her yielding form with scarce a bruise. Regaining her feet, she hastened back to the town, and soon was in her brother's arms.

The soldiers chased the panic-stricken Indians far over the prairie; and then, at last, growing weary of slaughter, the major checked the pursuit.

The sun was just rising as the little squad of troopers rode back into Tacos.

The lieutenant approached the major.

"There's ten of the Indians whose wounds I think are not mortal. I've had them taken into the little drinking-shop. I suppose we'll have to take them to Santa Fe as prisoners?" said Wenie.

"Yes; I will despatch a courier at once to Santa Fe, with an account of this affair. It's about the soundest thrashing that these marauding tigers have ever received along the border. They'll not be apt to make another raid across the Rio Grande, in this direction, for some time, I'm thinking."

"I'm afraid that our expedition to the brigands' retreat will have to be delayed another day," said Wenie, not feeling overpleased at the idea either. We will have to bury these dead redskins, and attend to our own wounded men as well as to the wounded Indians."

"That's true," replied the major. "Perhaps it is better as it is. In the meantime I may receive some information from my spy that will greatly aid our attack."

Though chafing at heart at the delay, yet the lieutenant calmly proceeded about his duties.

By afternoon, Tacos had resumed its wonted appearance, though here and there blood-stains on the walls and on the earth still bore witness to the terrible struggle.

Just as the dusk of evening was coming on, a Mexican rode into Tacos, and enquired for Lieutenant Wenie. He was speedily conducted to the lieutenant's quarters.

"Well?" said the lieutenant, as the Mexican, who was not remarkable for his good looks, appeared before him.

"You are Lieutenant Wenie?" asked the Mexican.

"Yes," answered Wenie.

"Will the senor look at this?" asked the man, drawing from his breast a little note.

The lieutenant's heart gave a leap of joy when his eyes rested upon the delicate inscription of the note, for he saw that it was Juanita's handwriting.

Eagerly he tore it open. It contained a single sentence—

"You may trust the bearer."

There was no signature, but each letter of the delicate handwriting was graven on Wenie's heart. He knew full well that the note was written by his beloved.

"Where is the lady?" the lieutenant questioned eagerly.

"At the hacienda of her father," answered the Mexican.

"Ah!" cried Wenie in joy; "she has returned then?"

"Yes; the senor brought her back this morning early and secretly," said the Mexican.

"How, then, did you know of her return?" demanded Wenie.

"The senor employed me to watch her."

"And you have betrayed your trust?"

"Yes, senor; I felt pity for the poor senorita. Besides, I am to have five golden ounces."

"If you can procure me an interview with her, you shall have ten," cried Wenie.

"If the senor find it out, I shall lose my place," said the Mexican.

"I'll find you another," replied the lieutenant.

"I promised the senorita to find you and tell you of her return; but to carry you back with me is dangerous."

"Remember, ten golden ounces," said Wenie.

The Mexican's eyes sparkled. Wenie renewed the temptation.

"Ten golden ounces will make a gentleman of you"

"Yes, senor."

"It is a fortune."

"Yes, senor."

"You accept?"

"Yes, senor."

"You are a worthy fellow!" cried Wenie, full of joy.

"Remember, I'm to have another place if the senor turns me off," said the Mexican.

"Yes, yes," replied Wenie.

"When do you wish to go?"

"At once."

"Impossible, senor. Remember, the hacienda is on a prairie; your approach could easily be seen. In an hour it will be dark. Cats can see in the night, not men."

" But there is a moon," said Wenie.

" The night will be cloudy," replied the Mexican.

" In an hour, then, you will come ?"

" I will wait here with the senor, if the senor will let me," replied the Mexican.

" Certainly !" cried Wenie, pacing rapidly up and down the floor, hardly able to conceal his impatience.

How slow, to Wenie's mind, the hour was in passing ! Never before had an hour seemed so long—never were the shades of night so tardy in descending !

To while the time away, Wenie questioned the Mexican as to whither Juanita had been carried, and as to the reason of this sudden return; but the Mexican knew nothing except that she had returned and had employed him to warn the lieutenant. He further explained that she was afraid to write more than the brief line for fear it might be discovered.

With this unsatisfactory account, the lieutenant was, perforce, obliged to be content.

Five minutes alone remained of the hour.

" Will you tell the boy to saddle my horse ? You will find him just back of the house," Wenie said to the Mexican.

After he had departed on his errand the lieutenant threw off his uniform coat, buckled a belt around his waist to which were attached two holsters, each carrying a revolver; then he slipped on his loose, undress coat and was prepared for the night adventure. Though apparently unarmed—the skirts of the coat concealing his revolvers—in reality he was fully prepared for danger. He had determined that if he could possibly carry off Juanita that night he would do so. He was ready now to do battle with a score for her sake.

Hardly had the lieutenant finished his preparations

when the Mexican returned, and after him came the servant with the horse.

Wenie leaped into the saddle, the Mexican mounted his mule, and the two set out.

As the Mexican had foretold, the night was dark. Heavy banks of clouds covered the sky; only now and then, at rare intervals, the moonbeams shone down upon the prairie.

"It looks like rain," said Wenie, as they galloped onward.

" The senor does not fear the rain?"

"Not on this errand," replied the lieutenant ; " a rain of liquid fire could hardly keep me back."

On rode the two. Tacos was left behind, and they galloped over the prairie. Already they had accomplished half the distance between the town and the hacienda, when something peculiar about his Mexican guide attracted Wenie's attention. A suspicion of treachery shot across his mind, for, lover though he was, yet his passion did not blind him; he was still the cool, cautious soldier. What it was about the guide that had excited his suspicion he could not tell, except that it was a stealthy kind of a watch that the Mexican seemed to be keeping ahead—a watch that he seemed to wish the lieutenant not to see.

Wenie resolved to be upon his guard. Cautiously he slipped his right hand—the Mexican was riding upon his left—under the skirt of his coat, and drew his revolver; as his arm was hanging down carelessly by his side, of course the Mexican could not see the weapon as they rode onward.

The hacienda was in sight. Wenie began to think his fears were foolish; a few minutes more and Juanita might be folded in his arms.

Just then they arrived at a little house that stood

by the road. As they reached it, the Mexican suddenly threw his arms around the lieutenant and essayed to drag him from the saddle; at the same moment five or six horsemen dashed around the corner of the house—which had concealed them from view—upon the two.

The truth flashed upon Wenie in an instant; it was an ambuscade.

Prompt was the lieutenant to act. Hardly had the arms of the Mexican closed around him ere the right hand, clutching the revolver, came down with crushing weight upon the Mexican's head. The grips of the arms relaxed and the treacherous dog tumbled out of the saddle. Levelling, Wenie fired at the horsemen approaching; two shots checked their advance and two saddles were emptied. The horsemen fired; the bullets whistled around the lieutenant's head; one struck him in the side and Wenie felt that he was wounded. Quickly he wheeled his horse and flew at the animal's topmost speed for Tacos. A volley from the pistols of the horsemen saluted his retreat; a ball pierced his shoulder.

The horsemen did not attempt to pursue him. It was plain pursuit was useless.

" Oh ! Satan protects him !" cried the leader of the assailants who was no other than the brigand chief, Ruy Lara.

The brigands looked to their wounded; one man, shot through the temple, was dead. The Mexican guide had only been stunned and was now recovering.

The other, who had fallen from the saddle at Wenie's fire, lay on the prairie groaning with pain; it was Tio.

" Are you badly hurt ?" asked Ruy.

" Yes," gasped Tio. " I'm shot through the lungs —leave me to die in peace," and with a convulsive gasp Tio sank back.

"Leave him to his fate," said Ruy, as he sprang into the saddle. "Poor devil! he insisted upon coming to-night though I never saw him eager for a fight before."

The brigands rode fast for their retreat.

Ruy's plan had failed ; longing for vengeance, he had resolved to kill or capture Wenie. The Mexican who had proved so treacherous to the lieutenant, had been admitted to Juanita's presence apparently secretly, and had offered to carry a message to her over. Juanita, little suspecting the haunt she was in, or the man she was trusting, had written the line that the crafty Ruy had used as a bait to lead the American lieutenant into the snare which Ruy had designed should prove his death.

And now, after all his plotting, the Mexican was riding homeward; his foe still alive—unharmed for aught he knew ; one more of his band had been killed and another lay dying on the prairie.

Bitterly the brigand cursed the evil fortune which seemed to surround him, but still more bitter would have been his curses could he have looked that night an hour later, into the quarters of Major Curtin, and seen the man who was conversing with the major there—who was apparently telling a pleasant jest at which the stern old soldier laughed long and heartily—the man was the spy who had just returned from the brigands' stronghold.

CHAPTER XV.
THE SURPRISE AT NIGHT

LIEUTENANT WENIE rode fast for Tacos; he felt some slight anxiety in regard to his wounds, for they might possibly be serious, although the pain was but trifling.

Arriving at Tacos, the lieutenant went at once to

the quarters of Major Curtin, and, briefly telling that astonished officer of the ambuscade that he had so luckily escaped, requested him to examine the wounds.

As the lieutenant had hoped, his hurts were but slight, and the major, who was something of a doctor, speedily dressed them.

"There," said the major, when he had finished; "in a week I'll warrant that hardly a trace of your wounds will remain."

"They will not prevent my going with the expedition to the brigands' stronghold, I hope?" asked Wenie, anxiously.

"Oh, no!" cried the major; "we'll start to-morrow, early."

"Very well," said the lieutenant. "I will retire to rest at once. I suppose I had better keep as quiet as possible."

"Decidedly; you'll have exercise enough to-morrow. I expect these fellow will show fight," replied the major.

The lieutenant proceeded at once to his quarters, and retired to rest.

The major again spread upon the table the rude map on which was traced the road that led to the brigands' retreat by the banks of the Rio Pecos. As the major bent over the map, he heard a knock at the door.

"Come in," said the major, a little impatient at being disturbed.

An orderly entered.

"What is it, O'Neal?"

"A man wants to see ye's, major," replied the soldier, saluting.

"What sort of a man?"

"A little yaller Mexican, sur."

"Well, show him in."

In a moment the stranger entered the room. The major cast the glance of his keen eyes upon him.

"Well?" asked the officer.

"The senor is Major Curtin?" asked the stranger, who was a wiry little Mexican, with eyes as keen as a rat's and as black as a jet bead.

"Yes," replied the major.

The Mexican then took from his girdle a little keen-edged knife; with the knife he proceeded to rip open the lining of his ragged jacket. The major watched the proceeding with interest.

From its hiding-place between the lining and the jacket, the Mexican drew out the letter.

"Will the senor look?" asked the Mexican, with a courtly bow, tendering the letter to the officer.

The major had already guessed who and what the stranger was, and so the contents of the letter in the bold hand of his excellency the Mexican President, did not surprise him.

After reading the letter, the major spoke.

"I presume, then, I have the pleasure of address-ing Senor Castello, Chief of Police of the city of Mexico?"

Yes, senor, replied the Mexican.

"You will pardon my want of courtesy in not offering you a chair," said the major, "but your strange dress—"

"Don't speak of it, senor. If I wear the dress of a beggar, I must not expect to be treated like a gen-tleman," said the Mexican, gracefully taking the offered chair. "But now to business. Of course, senor, you are aware that the president is as anxious to crush these Brigands of the Prairie, who plunder like your people and mine, as your Government;

and as it was extremely necessary, in order to make
the blow decisive, that someone should penetrate into their stronghold, and, knowing no one whom I
thought more fit for the office, I took it upon myself.
That is the reason, senor, why I became your spy
and you see me in these rags. I have just returned
from the brigands' stronghold, by the Rio Pecos."

" Ah, indeed !" exclaimed the major.

" You received a rude map a few days ago, tracing
out the route thither ?"

" Yes."

"I sent it to you," said the Mexican. "I did not
dare to bring it in person; for, of course, you are
aware, senor, that if the brigands had discovered my
object in seeking their haunt my life would have
been worth but little."

"It was indeed a mission of danger," replied the
major.

" True; but the reward if I succeed, is great,"
said the Mexican. " Then, besides, I like once in a
while to throw aside the cares of office; there is a
sort of pleasure in hunting human game; it reminds
me of what I was before I came under the notice of
his excellency General Santa Ana, who was graci-
ously pleased to elevate me to my present position."

" I had determined to attack the brigands to-morrow night," said the major.

" Good !" cried the Mexican; "I will lead you,
they will be like rats in a trap."

And so the officer and the spy arranged the details
of the expedition—the raid that was to bring death
or captivity to Ruy Lara and all his band.

The consultation finished, the Mexican bade the
major good-night, and left the house.

Hardly had the Mexican gained the street, when,
in the darkness, he ran against someone who was

passing. A moment the stranger looked into his face; then a cry of passion broke on the night air. A grip of iron encircled the Mexican's throat; backward he was cast to the earth, a knee upon his chest held him firm; before his eyes flashed the bright blade of a knife, that even now was uplifted to strike him in the throat.

Astonished at the unexpected assault, the Mexican had hardly made a motion of resistance—indeed, had he resisted to the utmost of his power, it would have availed but little against the muscular force of his unknown assailant.

"Dog of a brigand!" hissed a hoarse voice that the Mexican knew full well, "prepare for death. You were the guide that led my sister into the hands of her betrayer; now, Tio, see if your rat-like cunning will save you from my knife."

The voice was the voice of the Pathfinder; and the Mexican held beneath his knee was, indeed, no other than Tio.

Tio, whom we shall hereafter call by his proper name of Castello, had but feigned to be wounded when, on the prairie, he had fallen from his horse at the lieutenant's fire. Having procured all the information that he desired in regard to the brigands, his next movement was, of course, to impart that information to the commander of the United States forces in Tacos.

"I am not a brigand!" gasped Castello, hardly able to speak, from the grip of the Indian's hand upon his throat. "I am Major Curtin's spy!"

"The American's spy!" exclaimed Manuel.

"Yes, a spy," repeated Castello.

"If you are lying ——" said Manuel, fiercely.

"By the Virgin, I swear I speak the truth!" cried the Mexican. "Ruy Lara and his band are doomed"

D

" Are you speaking truth ?" asked Mannel.

" As I hope to be saved," replied Castello, not sorry to gain his feet and escape from the iron clutch of the peon. ,

" Doomed !" cried the Pathfinder. " Alas that they are not !"

" Say not so, brave Pathfinder," the spy responded ; " forty hours will bring destruction upon the Brigands of the Prairie."

" It is but the justice of heaven," returned the Indian.

" If you seek revenge upon Ruy Lara, ride with us to-morrow and you shall have it," said Castello. " The troops, indeed, will need the guidance of the Prairie Pathfinder."

" Good ; I will go with you."

And then the two parted.

—————

We will now return to the retreat of the brigands.

Lara and his men had returned from their unsuccessful expedition, cursing their ill-luck.

Torres listened to the tale of the lieutenant's escape with evident ill-humour.

" This North American has as many lives as a cat ; twice you have failed."

" The third time may be more successful," returned Ruy. " In the end I may triumph."

" That is true," replied Torres.

" Your daughter does not seem now to be any more favorable to me than she was before," said Ruy.

" Once your wife, she will learn to love you," replied Torres. " Ruy, you should have been my son, for I think of you as one."

" A strange way you have of showing it," responded Ruy. " You might have reared me an honest man, instead of making me what I am, a brigand and a villain."

"Years have changed my plans," the old man replied, slowly. "When I reared you in the school of vice I intended you but as a tool, an instrument of vengeance, which I was to use upon another's head, even if the struggle cost your life; but as you grew to manhood I learned to love you. I loved your mother once, boy; and your eyes are hers. Now I have given up all thoughts of vengeance—all thoughts of the vengeance that I meditated even before you were born. Now I will try and make you a better man. That is why I wish you to marry my Juanita; but I will explain more fully to-morrow. Good-night." And Torres left the apartment.

In his heart, Ruy Lara could not help confessing that he cared but little for the fair Mexican girl, Juanita. Another face was before his eyes; another love filled his heart. Rita, the peon girl—she it was who held captive the brigand leader.

"Shall I ever see her again?" he cried, passionately, as the remembrance of her beauty and truth rose up in his mind. And, with these gloomy thoughts the brigand captain retired to rest.

Two o'clock came. A new sentinel had taken his position; 'twas Legro.

Carbine in hand he paced up and down before the gate. Careless was his watch. He did not notice that a dark figure, which scaled the wall to the right of him and dropped noiselessly to the earth inside, was creeping cautiously towards him. On came the figure, slowly but surely, stealing forward with all the stealth of the panther. Hid by the shadow of the wall from the notice of the sentry, it came within six feet of the end of the little path that measured the beat; then the figure halted—waited until the sentinel turned his back, and then, with the quick dash of the hungry tiger, the Pathfinder sprung

·upon the brigand. The steel glittered for a moment in the air, then was driven to the hilt in the body of the ruffian, which fell heavily to the earth.

Manuel quickly opened the gate, and the soldiers, headed by Major Curtin and Lieutenant Wenie, poured in.

The surprise was complete. Taken defenceless in their beds, the brigands made but little resistance.

Among the prisoners was Ruy Lara.

Torres, rushing from his apartment, alarmed by the noise of the attack, had been struck by a random shot and mortally wounded.

When Major Curtin heard of this, he hastened to him at once.

The eyes of the dying Mexican gleamed with a strange lustre when he gazed on the face of the man he had hated so bitterly.

" Curtin," he said, slowly, for life was ebbing fast, " I have wronged you deeply."

"Make what amends you can while life is left you," solemnly replied the major, as he knelt by the side of the dying man.

" Your son, the child of Inez," gasped the Mexican.

"Does he live?" eagerly questioned the stern old soldier, now melted almost to woman's tenderness.

" Yes ; and——"

With his ear close to the lips of the dying man, the major listened to the story of the past.

CHAPTER XVI.
THE LOST SON.

WITHIN an hour from the time he received the wound, Torres, the Mexican, was dead.

Juanita, rising from the side of her dead parent, found consolation in the arms of her lover. There was now no obstacle to her union with the man she loved.

The expedition, with the captured brigands, returned to Tacos.

Major Curtin sat alone in his quarters; a sad look was upon the face of the old soldier. He sat with his head resting upon the table, supported by his hand.

"Let me see," he muttered; "the old Roman, Brutus, gave his son to death. Rome, his country, first, before ties of kindred. Am I a Brutus? No! no!" and the old soldier shook his head sadly.

The major's meditations were interrupted by the entrance of the orderly, O'Neal.

"A lady wants to see yez, major."

"Who is she?"

"Don't know, sur, but she looks as if she's been cryin'."

"Well, show her in."

The orderly withdrew, and a woman, with her face concealed in one of the shawls so common to the lower class of Mexican women, entered the room.

"Well, madam?" asked the major.

The girl removed the shawl and revealed the features of Rita, the peon girl.

"Oh, senor," she murmured, "Ruy Lara, I have been told that he is to die."

"It is likely," replied the officer.

"Oh, senor!" cried Rita, wringing her hands in anguish; "his death will kill me also!"

"Ah!" the major started; "you are called Rita, your brother has told me something about you and this unfortunate young man. You love him?"

"Yes, senor; love him better than life!"

"You would forsake home, friends, all for him?"

"Yes, senor—all!"

"This poor girl teaches me my duty," the major muttered between his teeth.

"Would you like to see this man?" he asked.

"Yes! yes!" answered the girl eagerly.

"Come with me, then," he said, casting over his shoulders a long cloak and putting on his hat.

Rita followed the major down the street until they arrived at the adobe house that held Ruy Lara a prisoner. A sentinel paced before the door.

The major and Rita entered.

Ruy, handcuffed, lay on a rude bunk in one corner of the room. The moonbeams, shining in through an opening in the wall, revealed to him the presence of his visitors.

"Rita!" he cried with joy, and in a moment the peon girl was folded to his heart.

The major stood quietly by and looked on.

"You will excuse me, senor," said Ruy; "but this girl is the only thing that I have in the world to love. She is the only creature on earth that loves me; can you wonder, senor, that I am glad to see her?"

"Are you prepared for death?" asked the major.

"Yes, senor; I have but one tie to bind me to the world—this love that has come to smile upon me in my prison and light my passage to the grave."

"Suppose by any chance you should escape death; do you think that, in the future, you would live a different life?"

"Yes, senor," eagerly replied Ruy; "I am not all bad, and I feel sure that this girl's love would make me a good man. I was never born for a brigand, but was made one by an uncle whose memory I detest."

The major took from his pocket a key and unlocked the handcuffs, as he said:

"Yes, I know of Torres and his great crime; know that he purposely wrecked your young life, but it is not yet too late to shake off the fate which his evil heart designed. Let what there is left of

nobility in your soul grow and you are saved—
saved !"

There were tears in the soldier's eyes, and his
voice was choked by emotion.

"Now, girl, you follow me; and you, sir, watch
your opportunity, when I engage the sentinel in conversation, to slip out through the door and down the
street; the shadow of the houses will conceal you.
At the end of the street wait for me."

The major went directly to the sentinel and
engaged him in conversation. Rita, standing near
the door, served as a mask for Ruy. A second
more, and Lara was at liberty, and gliding cautiously
down the street.

With a brief injunction to the sentry not to dis-
turb the prisoner, the major, with Rita, followed the
fugitive

At the end of the little street they found Ruy.

"Wait," said the old soldier, as he left them.

Clasped in each other's arms and lost in wonder,
the lovers waited the return of the old major.

In a short time the soldier returned, leading two
horses.

"Mount and fly," he said, briefly.

The moment they were in the saddle, he took Ruy
by the hand.

"Have you money ?" he asked.

"Yes," Ruy answered; "I have letters of credit
from Torres, on his banker in New Orleans, sewed
inside my jacket, besides some gold in my belt."

"Go, then, to New Orleans, and heaven speed
you," cried the major, grasping Ruy's hand warmly.
"Keep faith with this girl; lead an honest life, and
—you *will see me again!* Go, go! God bless you,
my soul!"

Off went the fugitives, wondering at the strange
manner of the old soldier.

Little did Ruy Lara dream that he was indeed the son of the American major—the child stolen by Torres when an infant. This was the secret that the dying Mexican had revealed to Curtin. This it was that had saved Ruy Lara.

The escape of the fugitive was discovered in the morning, but, as the major said carelessly that pursuit was useless, nothing was done.

Juanita and Wenie were married; true love met its reward. The lieutenant, throwing up his commission, took charge of the vast estates to which Juanita was heiress, and he soon became one of the men whom Texans were proud to honour.

The Brigands of the Prairie never recovered from their defeat; from that time forth they became a matter of history.

And the Pathfinder?

When he returned, a secret was given him to keep by the major. The secret removed the sting which had pierced to his very soul when he learned of Rita's flight with Ruy Lara. The marriage of Juanita for a while oppressed him; but the loving hearts of her and her devoted husband soon won him from his sorrow, and he became, thenceforward, the trusted agent and friend of the rich proprietor.

NED KELLY:
IRONCLAD BUSHRANGER.

Published Weekly, price One Penny. Half Yearly
Vol. 2s. 6d.

It is well known that for many years Ned Kelly had
made himself notorious by a series of crimes
wholly incompatible with the civilisation of the
nineteenth century. Ned Kelly's celebrated
steed, Marco Polo, is as well known at the
Antipodes as Dick Turpin's Black Bess in these
islands."—*Telegraph*, 7th July, 1881.

"It is notorious that the robbery of Mr.
Steward's corpse was mainly performed by the
assistance of NED KELLY'S BROTHER, the Captain of what was neither more nor less than a
pirate ship."—*Times*, July.

"The history of NED KELLY and his celebrated black horse, Marco Polo, will ever live
in the recollection of the Australian public.
The deeds of Dick Turpin, and the perfor-
mances of Black Bess, are tame beside those of
NED AND HIS NAG;' in addition to which
Ned's history is true, and Turpin's is pure
fiction."—*Press*, July.

106

Extract from CHAPTER CII.

Kelly was careful not to excite the suspicions of Joss too greatly.

He conversed in a bantering way with him, called for drinks, and smoked another cigar.

Mrs. Flynn seemingly took no notice. She appeared absorbed in the multitudinous ramifications of her business.

Presently the clock marked seven.

"Well, Joss, darlint, about that whisky?" she said, with an odd glint of the eye, which Kelly carefully observed.

"You rampagious she cat!" he thought to himself, "if I only had you safe."

But he simply watched Joss!

Kelly's object was to induce Joss to walk a few yards with him—to accompany him to a rendezvous, but how to do this had puzzled him sorely.

Morgan, however, suggested the means.

He wrote a letter from the "trap" with whom Joss had been in communication, and whose name he managed easily to learn, requesting Joss to meet him at the police-station upon important business.

Kelly managed so that the missive was delivered while he was at the bar, and chuckled with devilish glee as he saw him leave the house in answer to the letter, and walk blindfolded into the pit prepared for him.

"I shan't be long, Kelly," said Joss; "will you wait until I come back?"

"I don't care," answered Kelly, and reseated himself for a moment.

As soon, however, as the other's back was turned, he hastily rose and followed him; he took his way down a narrow street which led to the station.

Kelly followed him closely, but cautiously, until he came to a doorway at no great distance from an oystershop.

Kelly whistled, and out darted a party of seamen, who threw a horse-cloth over Joss's head.

Before he could shriek he was secured, and hurried along by his comrades.

It was quite dark, and by exercising great caution they managed to reach the boat that awaited them, into which Joss was bundled, far more dead than alive.

Meanwhile, at the police-station, several officers and some forty policemen had been selected for the expedition.

At first the officials refused to believe in the possibility of such audacity.

That a common bandit and bushranger should have the audacity to seize a vessel and sail round the world with his gang appeared in these modern times incredible.

(Let our readers who doubt this wait until they see what Kelly's brother did in this line, and the correspondence between Victoria and the British Government upon the subject, vide *Times*, July,1881).

Great was the joy, therefore, of the officers and men, at the prospect of such a wonderful capture.

Eight o'clock came, but no Joss, and the officers became very uneasy.

One of them determined to go down to the oyster-saloon and make enquiries.

Mrs. Flynn was very much alarmed. Her husband had gone out soon after seven.

The chief of the "robbers and thieves" was in the saloon, and he had gone after him.

"The scoundrel has had some hint!" cried the officer, and dashed back to the police-station.

Then all rushed to the shore, to see the supposed yaoht in the act of sailing out of the bay.

The officers were frantic with humiliation and rage. There was not a single steamer available for the chase ready.

All the men-of-war on the station were absent. cruising at sea.

It was determined, however, to send out a sharp revenue cutter to give warning.

But all felt bitterly disappointed at the failure of their well-laid scheme.

Meanwhile, Kelly and the whole of his band had got on board.

Joss was cast into the hold very tightly secured.

Kelly was determined to exercise a bitter vengeance upon the traitor.

It should paralyse even his own crew.

Now his principal object was to escape from his enemies.

That he would be hotly pursued he could well imagine, and safety was the first law.

A sharp look-out was kept, and then he and his men held a consultation.

Kelly determined to try him by court martial, condemn and hang him.

His associates were enraptured with the idea.

It was an idea suited to their ferocious natures. But for the timely action of Kelly they would all be lying in San Francisco jail.

Had the police but had the sense to keep Joss a prisoner all would have been over with them.

Death, or prison for life, would have been their portion without a doubt.

But they would soon have their revenge on the cowardly traitor who had turned upon his pals.

As soon as breakfast was over Kelly called those

who acted as officers together, and bade some of the men bring Joss in.

A court martial on board a regular ship is a very solemn thing.

If the weather be fine the ship is arranged with the greatest nicety.

The great cabin is prepared with a long table covered with a green cloth.

Pens, ink, and paper, prayer-books and the articles of war, are placed round to each member.

"Open the court," says the president.

In this case Kelly, Zeph, and Salmon Roe constituted the court, while pipes, tobacco, and spirits are placed before them.

The prisoner was brought in. He was deadly pale, and his legs shook under him with fright.

"So, you white-livered cur, you blooming son of a sea-wolf," cried Kelly, in a hoarse voice, "you sold us to the traps, did you?"

"I did not," retorted the trembling caitiff. "I never peached on a pal."

"You lie, you skulking hound," cried Kelly, as he drank off a glass of brandy. "I saw you come down the steps of the station; I heard you tell the trap you'd meet him at eight; I saw your look at your wife, you snivelling cur, going to see about the whisky."

"I tell you, Ned, it's false," faltered Joss. "My wife told me to be civil to the police, and tell 'em to look round; being civil to them don't do no harm."

"You spawn of —— fire, you hell-fire ca ., you skunk," answered Kelly, and for the benefit of the men who were listening, he told the whole story.

Groans and oaths emanated from all sides; execrations of the most fearful character.

"Now, boys, it's no use having any more palaver," he continued. "Guilty or not guilty?" he asked.

"Guilty!" was roared on all sides.

"And the penalty for peaching is——"

"Death!" replied all who were near.

Joss tried to speak, but he was dragged off to the deck, where during the brief trial all the needful preparations for the fearful execution had been made, but they fell far short of what Ned thought the merits of the case demanded.

Kelly, with a brutal laugh went down into the cabin, and tossed off a glass to his swift passage to a warm place.

Of course, according to these men and their villainous code, the deed was a just and retributive one.

He had been a traitor to his pals.

Kelly had for some days pondered over the form of death he would inflict upon

> "Yon trembling coward who forsook
> His master,"

as "My name is Norval" has it.

The yard-arm was too common, shooting was too sudden.

He must be done to death in a way to

> "Make the world grow pale,
> To point a moral and adorn a tale."

To make him an *auto defe*, to burn him on a pile like an Hindoo widow, to impale him and hang him "alive and kicking," up to the end of the yard-arm like a skewered kidney, there to linger out his days and nights in hopeless agony.

Each of these plans recommended themselves to the bushranger's idea of vengeance and justice.

But each had their objectionable points, and as the

trembling catiff stood before Ned he gave him his choice of the fate he would like best.

"Look here, you miserable, skulking, sneaking viper, I'm kind to you, I am, so we all are. You'd have handed us over to the traps. They wouldn't have been as kind to us as we are to you. They would not have given us the choice of how we'd be scragged. No, not they. Now make your choice. Which will you have—blazes, wood, or water? Look sharp, your time is short. We can't be nice about a hound that would have bitten us all and lapped up the blood-money. Speak, Joss, or I'll give tongue for you, and you'd better not leave that to Ned Kelly, I tell you."

"Roast the traitor who would have murdered us all—who sold his mates! Roast him! roast him!" rattled and roared out all the enraged men, who encircled the pallid, trembling, half-paralysed wretch, whose frightened eyes and quivering frame clearly photographed the apprehension that convulsed him.

He knew the men he stood before.

Their eyes were gleaming with vengeance—their hands eager to wreak it on the body of their would-be assassin. They stood glaring ferociously like wolves upon the shrinking wretch, while Kelly, like the presiding Satan, looked calmly and maliciously on, enjoying the torture that racked the frame of his victim.

Truly it was a scene where

> " Hope withering fled,
> And mercy sighed farewell!."

"Now, then, Joss, speak up ; tell the truth now if you never did before. Which shall it be—fire, wood, or water ?"

"Mercy—mercy, Ned!" gasped the horrified man. "Mercy for old times, Ned Kelly !"

"Yes, the mercy you'd have shown to Ned Kelly, when you thought to shunt him into the hands of Jack Ketch. Mercy—yes, the mercy you showed to your mates. What did they ever do to you, Joss—eh? Did they deserve to be murdered by their pal—oh? Answer me that."

The only answer was a groan.

"Finish the brute!" screamed the excited voices of the more excited listeners. "Lynch him! roast him! scrag him!" were the cries that raged like a tempest round the doomed man.

"Hold!" roared Kelly. "Listen to me," and all were silent as the grave. "He's not good enough for any of those forms of death. True men have been hung, brave men have been burnt, but dogs like Joss don't deserve the cost of a rope or a fire. No, my lads, he shall have a death only fit for such as him. We will lower him over the side and tow him after us as bait for the sharks, whose snouts are now, with true scent, following in our wake, knowing their dinner is preparing, and that death's aboard. We'll just dip him a bit, so that he shan't be gobbled up in a mouthful, but let him lose a leg first, then an arm, just to give him time to enjoy it."

This pleasantry was answered by a terrified shriek, and the poor devil fainted.

In the meantime everything was prepared,

A stout rope was tied round the upper part of his body, his arms and legs being left free.

When he came to, Kelly lifted the man in his powerful arms and carried him screaming to the side of the vessel.

The victim struggled all he knew how, with instinct of self-preservation, and without any hope of release. He felt his last terrible hour had come; what was more, he felt he deserved it.

His whole previous life passed in review before him; he suffered the pangs of death fifty times over. Verily, "The pains of hell gat hold upon him."

"Ain't I gentle, my baby?" mocked Kelly, as he quietly lowered the shrinking, quivering, trembling body over the side, by which the white-bellied sharks were coursing along their noses rising every minute above the water, as if anticipating the repast that was to fill their open jaws.

Shriek upon shriek issued from the unfortunate victim, as he turned his horrified gaze upon the formidable jaws of the huge beasts, who almost sprung from the waves to snatch the man from the arms that were lowering him to such a fearful and certain death.

Kelly held him with mock tenderness close to himself, laughing wildly and maliciously, as he almost cuddled Joss in his Herculean arms.

Those looking on, *almost* felt compunction, until the thought of the fate he had prepared for them re-awakened their vengeance, and stifled all human feeling.

Suddenly they were startled by a loud and furious curse, and Kelly was seen to grasp the man's throat.

Joss, in his despair and agony, had fixed his powerful teeth in the fleshy part of Kelly's arm, and held on like a tiger.

It was only when almost choked, that his bite relaxed.

Maddened by the pain, Kelly resolved the wretch's fate should not be postponed any longer, and crying out to those holding the tow-rope to " slack off," Joss was flopped into the water, which was soon reddened with blood, while half-a-dozen sharks soon obliterated all earthly sign of the once stalwart Joss.

Extract No. 2,

CHAPTER CXXVI.

BLACK BESS NOWHERE.

After glancing round, lest there should be any sign of danger, he alighted from Marco Polo's back, ascended the steps and rapped loudly at the door.

Again with no result.

"Hi, Appleby, blow you! By gosh, if you're not slippy, I'll burn your cursed old dog-kennel about your ears.'

"I don't think you will, sir," said a clear, ringing voice, close to his ear.

Ned glanced up in amazement.

A narrow slit had noiselessly opened a little to the right of the doorway, and through it protruded the barrel of a pistol which covered him completely.

But what still more surprised him was to mark that the hand holding the weapon was that of a woman, whose voice it was that had addressed him.

"Now then," she continued, in undaunted tones, "perhaps you'll tell me who you are and what you want."

With his usual recklessness he faced the speaker and replied—

"Well, my name happens to be Ned Kelly, and I want a roof, food, and fodder, not to mention the company of a pretty girl, if that's agreeable to you."

The slit was closed, and next moment Ned heard the fastenings of the huge outer door being undone.

Then it swung back, revealing on the threshold the figure of a young girl holding a light in one hand and a pistol in the other.

"Welcome, **Mr. Kelly**," she said, in the same confident tone.

She was a girl about eighteen or twenty, whom nineteen men out of twenty would have styled handsome, and ninety-nine women out of a hundred a fright.

"You're a clipping wench," was Ned's remark as he followed her into the hall, "but who the devil are you and what brings you here?"

The girl laughed.

"Well, I'm Appleby's daughter Jess, and I'm keeping house, you see."

"Ain't the governor at home?"

"No; he's off for a day or two on some lay or other."

"And left you here alone?"

"Why not? I reckon I can take care of the place and myself too," she said significantly.

Sooth to say Miss Jessie Appleby was in every way equal to the twofold task.

At sixteen Miss Jessie had emancipated herself from her aunt's care, and started life on her own account.

It is with deep regret we have to mention that in a very short time her career became of a somewhat prominent character, and led to her being brought into contact on several occasions with the Sydney police.

At length a little difficulty arising about a sailor who was found one morning on the pavement with his pockets turned out and his head caved in, led to her passing a twelvemonth in seclusion at the expense of Government.

On her release she judged a change of air advisable, and had accordingly come to act as housekeeper to her father at Lomax's old station.

"Well, you do seem a good plucked un," said Kelly in tones of unfeigned admiration.

" How about your horse?" asked the girl, paying no attention to the compliment. "There is very good shelter for him in the stable, it is better than it looks. Shall I light you to it?"

" No," answered Kelly with equal coolness, and an air as if the whole place belonged to him. 'Marco Polo and I don't care about being separated, and I guess I can find him quarters here."

Saying this he went out, and led the way up the steps into the large room which served as hall and dining and drawing room, all in one. Marco followed Ned like a pet-dog, and seemed no way surprised at his new quarters.

" Oh, what a beauty!" cried the girl in admiration.

" Yes, there ain't two like him under the southern cross," said Kelly, with equal enthusiasm.

" Get in there and make yourself comfortable," said Jess, indicating a large room opening off the right of the hall.

" No, no! beast before man in a case like this," was the bushranger's answer. " Marco's heels may have to save my neck before daylight, and looking after him is only taking care of number one. Is there any fodder on the premises ? "

" Plenty," answered Jess, leading the way to a back room.

Soon a corner of the hall was comfortably littered down for Marco Polo's reception, and, tired as he was, Ned proceeded to give the gallant animal a thorough rubbing down before leaving him to repose and the enjoyment of a feed of corn.

The girl aided him with approving eyes.

" You're the right sort," she observed, leading the way to the room she had already indicated.

Jessie proceeded to set food and drink on the table and called on him to fall to.

As he cast aside his broad hat before commenciuj his meal, and revealed his scarred and plaistered fac and the burnt stubble of his hair and beard, the gir gave a start of surprise.

Ned laughed.

"I don't look much of a beauty, do I?" said he.

"No, you don't."

"Oh! you see me at my worst. Just wait a weel or so, till my hair grows and I get rid of thes scratches, and I'll astonish you."

The girl sat down at the table, and the conversa tion between the pair soon became brisk and lively rather too lively, perhaps, for good taste.

Fatigue, a hearty meal, and two or three stif tumblers began, however, after a while, to have their effect on Ned, and he nodded once or twice in the chair.

"Pretty well done up, eh?" said the girl.

"Rather!" was the rejoinder. "I've got through a fair job of work since sunrise."

"Well, you'd better roll yourself up in a rug and take a coil on the ground."

Ned pondered for a minute.

But on reflection he came to the conclusion tnat Jessie was a girl to be trusted and, wrapping himself in the rug, stretched himself at full length on the floor, and was soon fast asleep, with his saddle under his head and his pistol gripped in his hand.

The hours passed on, the stars faded and the light of a new day began to steal over the plain, and still the robber slept and the girl watched over his slumbers.

Suddenly a shot, followed by a thundering noise at the outer door, made Ned spring to his feet, pistol in hand.

CHAPTER CXXVII.

"FIRST CATCH YOUR HARE."

WHEN Sergeant Whitwell found the trick that had been played on him by Kelly at the ford, his fury knew no bounds.

To be done in any way was bad enough, but to be made to look small in the eyes of those subordinates to whom he had been laying down the law, was unbearable.

In his heart he cursed Kelly, and vowed if ever he had the chance of a shot at him he would not hesitate.

After blowing off as much steam as he could in abusing Anderson, upon whom he laid the whole blame, and whom he threatened to put under arrest, he proceeded to resume pursuit.

It was a work of no small difficulty to find Ned's trail, and to follow it to the swamp.

"Is there a chance of getting hold of a black fellow, hereabouts?" he enquired of Sam.

"Well, there are one or two hang about Eldred's station," replied that worthy. "There's a shepherd's hut somewhere about a couple of miles to the northward, and I fancy he might be able to help us."

Sam and one of the troopers were despatched in quest of this worthy, the rest of the party endeavouring to follow Ned's trail, which was by no means an easy job, as it was lost in the marshy ground.

Finally they had to give it up, and await the return of their messengers.

At length these made their appearance, accompanied by the shepherd and a black boy of about sixteen, and provided, moreover, with a lantern.

Night was indeed fast coming on.

The black, like all his tribe, had a great objection

to be abroad in the dark, but threats, promises, the company of white men, and the light, helped to overcome his terror.

So soon as the black was made, with some difficulty, to comprehend the dodge Kelly had practised upon his pursuers, he directed the party to separate, and skirt the marshy swamp into which Kelly's tracks were followed, and thus find the spot at which he had debouched and started squarely on his journey.

The black's advice was immediately followed, the sergeant imprecating his own stupidity in not having thought of this self-evident proceeding instead of not being indebted to a " nigger " for the suggestion. The police divided their forces, each taking the half-circle skirt round the edge of the swamp.

Keeping a good look-out (the moon shining as it only does shine in Australia, and illuminating the ground as clearly as an English sun) the said "nigger" was the first to detect the marks of Marco's hoofs, which important fact he heralded by loud guttural chuckles, and exclamations of "Yarrow-yarrow, quam by here!" (Horse marks here.)

"Got him at last, by Jingo!" shouted the sergeant, exultingly. "Now, my beauty, if I don't run you to earth and get a pile for your brush, why, my head's only fit for cat's meat."

"I should say, sergeant," said Casson, "from the course he has evidently taken, that he's making his way to Lomax's old station. That chap, Appleby, who's squatting there now, is a bad egg, if ever there was one, and would be sure to help him."

"That's about it," answered Whitwell. "Come, we can push on pretty smartly. There's no doubt but that's where he's making for."

They stuck to Marco's tracks, which the black followed like a beaten road.

Despite their hurry, however, it was broad daylight before the old station stood revealed to them in all its desolation.

Before they approached it they halted, and a kind of council of war was held.

The black refused to advance any further.

In common with his tribe he firmly believed the spot haunted by the ghost of Lomax, and neither threats nor promises could induce him to venture within its clutches.

The shepherd was, he frankly admitted, a non-combatant, and Master Sam showed a decided reluctance to trusting his ugly carcase within pistol-shot of the man he had betrayed to the police, and whom he knew was a dead shot at twenty paces.

The five troopers resolved therefore to surround the house, after first riding round it in a wide circuit with the black, in order to verify the fact that there was no trail leading away from the station.

Dismounting and leaving their horses under the care of Sam and the shepherd, they stole cautiously forward to the main building.

Reconnoitring, they ascertained that there were only two entrances, one in front and one in the rear.

The sergeant stationed two of his men at the back of the house, with orders to shoot down Kelly if he attempted to break away in that direction, or if he sought to escape by the side windows.

Then with the other two he quietly ascended the steps of the verandah.

"If he's here," he observed, "we shall nab him to a certainty."

And placing the muzzle of his carbine to the key-hole he blew the lock to flinders

After which, he and his comrades commenced a vigorous assault on the door with the butt-ends of their carbines.

It might have been more in accordance with the laws of warfare to have summoned the garrison to surrender; but the sergeant, knowing from Marco's tracks up to the house that Ned was within, thought any such courtesy superfluous.

The bars held firm, however; and for some time the thundering din produced no response.

Suddenly a hoarse voice was heard within, demanding who the devil it was hammering at the door in that fashion.

"All right, Master Kelly," cried Whitwell. "Just open the door and let us in, or we'll find a way to smoke you out of your hole."

A laugh was the only answer.

"Hammer away, lads," cried the sergeant. "We'll have this door down in a brace of shakes, and then that joker'll laugh on the wrong side of his mouth."

Suddenly the panel in the shutter flew open, a pistol shot rang out, and, with a low moan, the sergeant dropped in his tracks."

Before the other two could well realise whence the attack came, a second shot was fired, the ball passing through Whitwell's arm, and, ere he and his companions could turn their carbines against their foe, the panel was re-closed.

A panic seized them, and, fairly turning tail, they trotted from the verandah like startled rabbits, and did not halt till they had gained the shelter of the ruined outbuildings.

Another shot, and a cry from their companions in the rear of the house, warned them that they, too, were in equal peril, and next minute they saw them falling back.

Ere, however, they could gain shelter, a fourt shot was fired from the house, and the bullet lodgin in Casson's leg brought him to the ground.

Holmes, his companion, seized him in his arme and, swinging him on to his shoulder, succeeded i bearing him out of range.

Matters were evidently critical.

With two of their number *hors de combat*, and : third wounded, their chance of capturing Kelly seemed farther off than ever.

Holmes and his wounded companion having re-joined them, they took counsel.

"Look here," said Whitwell, whose wound on ex-amination was found not to be so serious as they had at first imagined, "we must turn this siege into a blockade. We can't storm the house, but the fellow inside is in an equally tight fix, for if he ventures into the open we can knock him over like a rabbit."

"That's so," said Holmes.

"Well, all we've got to do is to keep a sharp look-out, and, meanwhile, send back the shepherd for help."

"Yes, that's all very well," growled Anderson, whose temper had not been improved by the ser-geant's rating concerning his oversight at the first, "but if the captain comes up with the rest of the police, he'll get the reward, and we shall run all the risk in the meantime."

"Something in that," remarked Holmes.

"I don't like this job over much," resumed Ander-son. "If five of us couldn't come to the end of the fellow, I'm blessed if I see how two and a half, for that's all we are, can. How are we to keep watch on all sides of the house?"

"Oh, as for that," said Casson, pluckily. "I am not quite done for My leg hurts awful, but I think

I could manage to shoot straight, in spite of it. **Only**
let me have a fair crack at that beggar, and I'll
lay odds he won't forget me."

"But how about the sergeant?" asked Whitwell.
"I don't think he's dead."

"Ain't there a way of luring Kelly out into the
open?" said Holmes. "If we could only manage
that, we could bowl him over easily. He's got no
horse."

"Where the devil has he hid his horse?" asked
Anderson.

"Somewhere in these sheds, I expect. Hullo!"

This last remark was called forth by a startling
incident.

About fifty yards intervened between the shed in
which they had ensconced themselves and the dwell-
ing-house.

Suddenly the door of the latter opened.

They sprang to their arms, expecting to see the
form of the bushranger cross the threshold.

Instead of this, however, they merely saw a pole
fitted at the end with a hook, thrust forth by some
invisible hand.

Before they could advance, the hook was fastened in
the garments of their fallen leader, the sergeant; he
was jerked swiftly into the house, and the door was
again closed.

Two minutes later, the same pole with a dirty
white apron fastened to the end was thrust through
the panel and waved in invitation.

"It's a flag of truce," said Holmes.

"Who's going to answer it?" asked Anderson.

"Why, I don't mind, said Whitwell, pluckily. "I
am hit already, and it would be better for me to come
to grief than one of you fellows. Besides, I believe
Kelly will keep his word."

124

Fastening his handkerchief on the end of a stick, Whitwell advanced towards the door.

"Stop there!" yelled Ned, as soon as he was within ten yards of the door, "or I'll fire at you."

"What do you want?" asked the undaunted trooper.

"I want to know how long you fellows are going to keep loafing about the premises," was the jeering answer.

"Till you come out."

"If I do come out I'll give you a lesson you won't forget in a hurry. But I'm willing to do it."

"Oh!"

"Yes, if you'll give me a chance."

"What do you mean?"

"Why, just this. In the first place, I've got your serjeant in here."

"Well?"

". Well, he ain't dead, but I tell you he blessed soon will be unless you give me a chance of bolting. And I'll tell you something more; if you don't give me the chance I ask for, I'm blessed if I won't burn him alive over a slow fire before you get in this crib."

"Go on."

"It's just this. I'm not going to wait till you've sent off and aroused the country, which will be your little game next, I guess."

"Oh, you're as deep as a lawyer, you are!"

"Right you are. Now, what I want is this. You and your mates shall fall back a hundred and fifty yards from the house. I don't think there's any chance of your hitting me at a hundred and fifty yards," he continued reflectively, "but to make matters quite safe we'll say two hundred."

"One of us is wounded and can't walk."

"Well! he can stay."

"What next?"

"Your horses must be tethered out of sight, so that they cannot be brought up to you before I get my start. Say yes or no. Sharp's the word. Niether Ned or the sergeant shall be taken alive."

"I will fall back and consult my comrades. I see nothing to disagree with, myself; and if they agree, I'll step out and wave this flag twice. You must trust me."

"I know I can. You are a brave fellow to trust youself within pistol-shot of me, and I know you're the sort to keep your word."

Whitwell rejoined his comrades, and after a brief consultation it was agreed to accept Ned's terms.

It was evident he wanted to get a start, and trust to his fleetness on foot to escape into the neighbouring scrub.

But they felt sure of baffling him.

Holmes proceeded to the men in charge of the horses, which were grouped on a little knoll some five hundred yards to the left of the house.

In obedience to his orders, Sam, the shepherd, and the black fellow picketed their chargers, and then fell back a hundred yards further.

Holmes rejoined his companions, and after Whitwell had stepped forward and waved his flag as a signal, the whole, with the exception of Casson, fell back to the distance indicated.

The position was then as follows:—

The troopers were two hundred yards in front but to the left of the house.

Their horses were five hundred yards behind them

Consequently, they were about three hundred yards apart.

Kelly, on the other hand, was only two hundred from the advanced guard.

But then the shepherd, Sam, and the black fellow, were only a hundred yards from the horses, and their orders were, directly the door opened to run like the wind to them and gallop off with them to the troopers, who would surely be able to overtake Kelly who, on foot, could not keep up racing-pace very long.

Meanwhile, Ned had completed his preparations.

After despoiling the insensible sergeant of his uniform, he had locked him in the room in which he had himself passed the night.

Then saddling Marco Polo he led him quietly up to the front door.

He softly undid the bars.

Jessie was watching him with the utmost interest.

" Now, lass, it's your turn," he said.

She evidently understood him, for she stepped forward with a couple of silk handkerchiefs in her hand.

One of these he proceeded to tie over her mouth, after bestowing upon her lips a hearty smack which she seemed by no means reluctant to receive.

With the other he tied her hands at the wrists, leaving, however, the fingers at full liberty.

Then he got into Marco Polo's saddle, cocked his revolver, that belonged to the sergeant, and crouched flat on the horse's neck.

" Now ! " he said.

The would-be captors of Kelly were in an agony of expectation and excitement, expecting to see the redoubtable bushranger walk into the net, but they little knew the resource and ingenuity of the man they thought was within their grasp. They remembered that the fellow seemed to bear as charmed a life as that of Macbeth, who was to be slain by—

" No man of woman born ! "

He had been shot at, but stood invulnerable, the bullets rattling off his body as harmless as peas off a crocodile's back. His enemies little knew that they wasted their pellets upon an "ironclad," for Kelly always wore in these encounters a suit of mail, hammered out of ploughshares, which rendered him bullet-proof. With open mouth and strained eyes they stared at the door by which they expected to see Ned escape. They were not long kept in suspense. Suddenly the door was rapidly thrown open, and disclosed Kelly mounted on Marco Polo, who the next moment was seen to clear the steps at a bound, with his tail as straight as a fence in a gale of wind, and his eyes as bright as lightning-flashes, as if he knew he bore Cæsar and his fortunes on his back. Whew! on he came, as Jonathan would say, like greased lightning, Kelly's loud, defiant laugh ringing out clearly, while, waving his hat triumphantly, he chaffed his enemies with cutting sarcasm to "come and take him," to "get up behind," and promising to square up with Sam before many months were over that worthy's head.

Down and over the steps, as if he were taking a stream in his stride, the gallant animal answered the heel and hopes of his daring rider, who, with a pistol in his grasp cocked and ready for action, galloped to where the police horses were tethered, and drawing the policeman's sword, with which, as with his uniform, he was furnished, proceeded with a few furious slashes to hough—in other words, to hamstring—the unfortunate brutes, and thus render pursuit for the present impossible. The troopers looked on perfectly stupefied, and, if truth must be told, not a little dismayed. They knew that if able to come up with Kelly while engaged in the barbarous, but to him necessary, onslaught, the foremost arrivals would certainly be "dead meat," and Kelly's escape (being mounted) not prevented.

|

www.ingramcontent.com/pod-product-compliance
Lightning Source LLC
Chambersburg PA
CBHW020754020726
47495CB00008B/2420